TEARS OF BLOOD

By
Raymond Warrillow

ISBN 978-1-909435-42-1

TEARS OF BLOOD

Chapter One

Nicole Morgan was travelling home on the bus. She lived in Birchfield, Birmingham. She was nineteen, had a shapely figure, and was pretty. She wiped the bus window with a paper tissue so that she could see outside. It was raining, and it was her stop. She stood up and climbed off the bus. Why did it rain every time she had her hair done? She opened her umbrella, and the wind blew it inside out. "Blast it." She pushed the broken umbrella into a bin, put her handbag over her head and ran along the pavement. The rain was crashing down.

By the time she had crossed over the road and run up the path to her front door, she was as soaked as if she had been for a swim. Having her hair done had been a total waste of time and money. She opened the door and stepped into the hall. She had hoped to look nice for her date with Tom. She looked in the mirror. Her hair was plastered to her head.

Her mother, Pat, walked into the hall from the kitchen. She looked shocked. "Good heavens, Nicole. Why didn't you take your umbrella?"

"I did. It broke." She took off her coat. "I'm supposed to be going out with Tom, and look at me."

"Do you want me to cook you a meal?" her mother asked.

"No. I won't have time. I've got to have a shower and do something with my hair." She looked at her watch. "Tom's picking me up in forty minutes."

"I'll make you a cup of coffee," her mother said. "I'll bring it up."

Despite being soaked by the rain, Nicole was happy. She was falling in love. Tom Dixon was made for her. He was twenty-five, tall, muscular and the most handsome man she had ever met. He was also fun to be with. They had been going out together for three weeks. She had now decided to have sex with him. It would be her first time, and she was feeling nervous.

She showered, dressed and did what she could with her hair.

Her mother walked into the bedroom and pointed to a cup of coffee on the dressing table. "You've let your coffee go cold. Do you want me to make you another cup?"

"No, thanks. I won't have time to drink it."

Her mother sat on the bed. "You got ready in record time."

Nicole stared at her reflection in the mirror. "I think I might have my hair cut. It's more trouble than it's worth."

"Don't you dare," her mother said. "You have beautiful hair." Her mother was forty-eight and had given up trying to look attractive. She wore cardigans and rarely wore makeup.

"I was only joking," Nicole said.

"I should hope so. You're seeing a great deal of Tom. He's a nice young man, but be careful."

"I'm always careful. Do you like him?"

Her mother nodded. "Yes. Your father likes him as well. Is he keen on you?"

"Yes, and I'm keen on him." Someone knocked on the front door. "That'll be him now."

Her mother stood up. "Your father will let him in."

Nicole picked up her handbag, checked her reflection in the mirror and walked down the stairs. Tom was talking to her father, Andy, about the weather.

"There's more rain forecasted, so be careful," Nicole's father said to Tom. Nicole's father looked young for his fifty-five years. He still had a full head of hair and was only a little overweight.

"I will," Tom said. He grinned at Nicole. "I've brought my golfing umbrella so you won't get soaked walking to the car. It's tipping down."

"That's very considerate of you, Tom," Nicole's mother said as she followed Nicole down the stairs.

"I aim to please," Tom said.

They said goodbye to her parents, and she managed to get into Tom's car with only her feet getting wet. "If it keeps raining like this, the river behind my house will flood into our back garden," she said.

Tom pulled Nicole into his arms and kissed her on the lips. She could spend the entire evening in his arms. His kisses sent her pulse racing.

He released her, started the car and drove down the road. "I've been thinking about you all day. You're the most beautiful woman I've ever met. How would you like to go on holiday with me?"

"I usually go with my friends. Where were you thinking of going?"

"To Glasgow. I'll be working there in three weeks. We could spend every evening together." He squeezed her knee. "And we could sleep together. We've known each other for nearly a month, and I've only had a feel."

"I don't jump into bed with men. I like to be sure of the man first."

He glanced at her. "I'm dead keen on you. I've never felt like this about a woman before. Is there any chance that we could sleep together?"

"There might be. I'm also keen on you."

"When? How about tonight? I can park the car on a side road."

"I'm not having sex in the back of a car." It would be her first time, and she wanted it to be special.

"I'll book us into a hotel," he said. "I know just the place. I'm working this weekend, so it will have to be Monday. We can spend the night together."

She would love to spend the night with him. "Why can't we go to your flat?"

"No way. It's a dump. I intend to find a decent place. I've been looking at this two-bedroom flat in Knowle. We could live together."

She smiled. "There's no need to rush things."

"I'll be honest with you," he said. "I've never thought about marriage until I met you. You're exactly the sort of woman I would like to settle down with. We would make a perfect couple."

She was pleased that he was keen on her. "Are you proposing to me?"

"Yes. I want you to know how serious I am about you."

"I'm only nineteen, and I don't intend to get married until I'm at least twenty-five."

"We could live together," he said. "We would then be able to really get to know each other."

"When we've been going out together for twelve months, I'll think about moving in with you."

They went for a drink in The Figure of Eight public house and talked about their lives. He had no brothers or sisters, and his parents had died in a car accident. He had spent two years working in New York and twelve months in France. He worked on computers and could speak fluent French. He used to play rugby until he hurt his knee. She felt that she was beginning to get to know him.

He drove her home, and they spent fifteen minutes kissing in his car. She was very aroused and was looking forward to Monday night. She pulled his hands away from her breasts. "It's time I went in. I need my beauty sleep."

"You're beautiful enough," he said. "I'll pick you up at eight on Monday."

"Yes. Bye."

She climbed out of his car and ran up the path. The rain had almost stopped. She was high with happiness. He had almost proposed to her, and so must also be falling in love with her. She hoped so. She was already in love with him.

*

Brad Croft could not make up his mind which woman to go out with. He was walking towards The Plough public house in Birmingham with a beautiful woman on each arm. They were sisters and were chatting away non-stop. Kelly Timms and her sister, Emma, were both tall, slim and pretty with short blonde hair. They were also fun to be with. The difference between them was that Kelly had a larger bust, and Emma had shapelier legs and a perfect bum.

"Which of us are you going to take out?" Kelly asked. "We're both mad about you."

"How can I take one of you out without upsetting the other?" He was twenty-two, six feet two inches tall, muscular, had dark hair, and was handsome.

"Then take us both out," Emma said. "Take me out next Saturday, and Kelly the following Saturday. We're used to sharing boyfriends."

He smiled. "Okay. It's a date."

They walked into The Plough public house, and he sat down next to his mates, Paul Evans and Mark Hill. They were both twenty. Paul was tall, slim, and average-looking. Mark was short, stocky and ugly.

"We're celebrating tonight," Paul said. "I intend to get legless."

"What are you celebrating?" Brad asked. "We lost five-three on Sunday."

"We've got our A-level results," Mark said. He put his arm around Paul's shoulders. "We've both got the required grades, and we'll soon be off to Leeds University."

"You could have been going with us, Brad, if you hadn't dropped out," Paul said.

"I couldn't stand the maths," Brad said. "I'm thinking of doing a business A-level." He was envious of Paul and Mark. He had always dreamed of going to university.

His mates slowly got drunk, and Brad began to feel depressed. Why was he wasting his life? He was a salesman at a sports shop in Solihull and hated every minute of it. He had the brains to get A-levels if he made the effort. By the time he was on his fourth drink, he had vowed to get English and business study A-levels and join Paul and Mark next year at Leeds University.

Brad was pulled to his feet and forced to dance with Emma. He was not in the mood. "I don't feel like dancing."

"Why?"

"I'm feeling a bit down."

"What you need is an ecstasy tablet," Emma said. She pressed something into his hand. "You'll then feel like dancing the night away."

A short time later, he stopped dancing and sat down. He had never taken drugs. He opened his hand and looked at the tablet. It might do him good. He was feeling depressed, and the lager was not lifting his spirits. One ecstasy tablet should not do any harm.

He popped the tablet in his mouth and swilled it down with lager.

While Paul was telling a joke, Kelly and Emma sat down at their table.

"I feel horrible," Kelly said.

"So do I," Emma said. "It must be something we ate."

"It's the drugs you keep taking," Mark said.

Kelly slid off her chair and fell to the floor.

"Fucking hell," Paul said.

As Paul tried to lift Kelly back onto her chair, Emma collapsed.

"I bet they've taken drugs," Mark said. "I'll phone for an ambulance."

Brad stood up. He began to panic. He had taken the ecstasy tablet that Emma had given him. If the ecstasy tablet had made them ill, he was in serious trouble. He ran into the toilet, pushed his fingers down his throat and was sick. He leaned against the sink and took a deep breath as relief flooded through him. A small white tablet was floating in the sick.

He looked in the mirror. His worried face stared back at him. "You fucking idiot." He began to worry about Kelly and Emma and ran out of the toilet and into the lounge. Kelly and Emma were lying on the floor, and Paul and Mark were kneeling by them.

"They look to be in a bad way," Brad said.

Paul stood up. "The fucking idiots. I told them a dozen times to steer clear of drugs. It would be all right if the drugs were pure. You have no way of knowing what some idiot might have put into the drug."

Two paramedics ran into the lounge and began to examine Kelly and Emma.

"Does anyone know if they've taken any drugs?" one of the paramedics asked.

"They have both taken an ecstasy tablet," Brad said.

"The fools," the other paramedic said.

The two sisters were put on stretchers and carried out of the public house. Brad and his two mates sat down at the table. Brad was even more depressed and slowly got drunk. It was the first and the last time he would ever take drugs.

*

Nicole was shopping with her mother in the centre of Birmingham. She bought a new outfit for Monday night and some sexy underwear.

Her mother frowned. "Why don't you get proper knickers? It would aggravate me to have a strip of material in my bum."

Nicole smiled. "All young women wear thongs today." She almost added that men find them attractive.

Her mother was obsessed with cafés, and they once again stopped for a coffee in the Pavilion.

"I love shopping in Birmingham," her mother said. "I'm glad you came with me today. I hate shopping on my own. Your father hates the traffic and will only drive to Solihull. He can be so stubborn."

As they were leaving the café, Tom walked in. He was with a woman and two little girls. He was holding the little girl's hands.

"Can I have an ice cream, Daddy?" one of the little girls asked.

"Yes, if you behave yourself," Tom said.

"We'll sit here, Tom," the woman said.

Nicole looked away. She was shocked. Tom was married and had two little girls. The man she had fallen in love with was a lying cheat.

The ride home on the bus seemed to take forever. Nicole felt confused and hurt. Why had he lied to her? What was wrong with men? Why can't they be satisfied with one woman?

She held back the tears until she was in her bedroom. She lay on her bed and sobbed. The tears eventually stopped, and she sat on the side of her bed. Tom had seemed so decent and honest. If she had not seen him with his wife and children, she would have had sex with him. She now realised why he only saw her during the week. She began to feel angry. She picked up her mobile phone and phoned him.

"Hello, Nicole," Tom said.

"I won't be seeing you again," she said.

"Why? What's wrong?"

"You're married."

"I'm not."

"You are. I saw you with your wife and two children."

"Fuck it," he said. "It doesn't change anything. I'll explain."

"How can you explain away a wife and two children?"

"I'm getting a divorce. I'll explain everything on Monday night. I've already booked the hotel."

"I won't ever be seeing you again. You're a lying, cheating bastard."

"At least let me see you to explain things," he said. "I've already left my wife."

"I wish I had never met you, and don't phone me again; otherwise, I'll have a word with your wife."

"Go and get fucked," he said. "You're nothing but a stuck-up bitch."

She ended the call and lay on her bed. How could she have been fooled by him? How could she have believed that he was a decent man? From now on, she would not go out with a man on a second date until she had spoken to his mother to make sure he was not married.

*

Brad had bought two bunches of flowers to give to Kelly and Emma. He now felt guilty about not going to the hospital with them. When he saw them, he was going to try to persuade them to give up drugs. His phone hummed. He took it out of his pocket. It was Paul. "Hello."

"Have you heard?"

"Heard what?"

"Kelly's dead. I've just found out. Emma's recovered and gone home. I can't believe it. The police said that there was something wrong with the drugs they took."

Brad was shocked. "Dead. Fucking hell."

"I'll see you tomorrow," Paul said. "The kick-off's at ten-thirty. Don't be late."

"I won't." Brad put his phone in his pocket and stared at a bee buzzing around the bunches of flowers. He could not believe that Kelly was dead. He shoved the flowers in a bin and walked off. He needed a drink.

He sat down with a pint of lager at a table outside the Greyhound public house and had a long drink. His thoughts were flying all over the place. Kelly was dead. It did not seem possible. What shocked him even more was that he had taken an illegal drug. What the fucking hell had he been thinking? He had always called drug takers fools.

He lit a cigarette and leaned back in his seat. If he had not forced himself to be sick, he might also be dead. He imagined the police telling his parents that he was dead and that he had been taking drugs. He closed his eyes and shook his head. It would kill them. This was a wake-up call. He needed to sort his life out.

What did he really want out of life? Getting drunk and playing football was not enough. Eventually, he would like to get married and have a couple of kids, but first, he would need to get a decent job. He was now more determined than ever to get a couple of A levels and go to university.

Chapter Two

It was Wednesday afternoon. Brad was sitting on a bench in the centre of Birmingham. He was feeling depressed and regretted going to Kelly's funeral. Not because he had been sacked for having the day off; it was seeing Emma and her parents crying that had upset him. They were standing by the side of Kelly's grave with their arms around each other, sobbing their hearts out. It had upset him more than he would like to admit. Unless it was a member of his family, he had no intention of ever going to another funeral.

A young woman walked past him. She had the kind of figure he liked, shapely and sexy. She was going his way, and so he followed her. He wanted to know what she looked like. She had a sexy walk but was probably as ugly as sin. She stopped at a bus stop, and he walked past her. She was smiling and texting someone on her phone. She was beautiful. He stopped. He had never seen such a beautiful woman before.

He stood watching her. She was probably a conceited bore, but she might be as beautiful on the inside as she was on the outside. No, that would be asking for too much, but you never know. She looked the decent sort. He had been telling himself for months to get a decent girlfriend, so he decided to ask her for a date.

Nicole looked up. A young man had stopped in front of her.

"I'm feeling really upset," he said.

She frowned. "Why are you upset?"

"I've just found out that Father Christmas isn't real."

She smiled. He was very handsome. "What sort of chat-up line is that?"

He spread his hands. "When I saw you, I had to talk to you, and it was the best I could do on the spur of the moment. Are you an Emma or a Jackie?"

Nicole was chatted up every day, and she would usually say that she had a boyfriend. "My name's Nicole."

She was looking at him as if she liked him, and so he decided to jump in the deep end. "How about going for a drink with me, Nicole?"

"I don't go out with men I don't know." She was tempted to go out with him. He was very good-looking and seemed like a nice person.

"If we go for a drink, we could get to know each other," he said.

If she said no, she would never see him again, so she decided to take a chance and hope that he was not married. "When?"

"Friday. I'll meet you at eight outside the museum and art gallery."

"I might be there," she said.

"I hope you will be there. "What job do you do?'

"I'm a student at Aston University." Her bus stopped at the stop, and she climbed aboard. "I'll see you on Friday at eight."

He grinned. "Don't be late."

*

It was five o'clock on Friday afternoon. Nicole felt exhausted. She was on the top floor of Aston University, having a private violin lesson with her tutor, Lucinda Evans. It was very hot, and even though she was standing by an open window, she was finding it difficult to breathe. She was also finding it difficult to concentrate, and Lucinda knew it.

Nicole took the violin from under her chin and smiled at the wrinkled face of Lucinda. "I'm sorry, Lucinda. I didn't get that quite right, did I?"

"I'll say you didn't. It sounded like a dying cat. If I didn't know better, I would say you were in love."

Nicole was amazed. Lucinda was very near to being right. "I'm not in love, although I am meeting a young man this evening."

Lucinda smiled. She was seventy-five, small and thin. "I might be an old lady, but I know all about falling in love." She looked at her watch. "I think we'll call it a day."

Nicole put her violin into its case and breathed a sigh of relief. She was not in the mood to concentrate. "Did you ever fall in love, Lucinda?"

"Yes. I fell in love three times."

"Then why didn't you get married?" Nicole asked.

"I did. I got married three times. I have three sons. One from each marriage. They're all grown up now with families of their own. One lives in Ontario, another in Tokyo and the youngest in Canberra."

Nicole was surprised. "If you've been married, why are you called 'miss'?"

"By choice. I also changed my Christian name to Lucinda. Would you like to know what my mother named me?"

"Yes."

"Mabel. I hated it."

"I must admit that I like Lucinda better than Mabel," Nicole said.

"I had the Mickey taken out of me when I was at school," Lucinda said. "There used to be a radio programme where Wilfred Pickles said, 'What's on the table, Mabel?' Every week, someone would say to me, 'What's on the table, Mabel?' It drove me mad, so I changed my name by deed poll." She opened the door. "Off you go. I'll see you on Friday afternoon, and I hope you'll be able to concentrate then."

"I will," Nicole promised as she stepped out of the room. "Bye."

"Bye," Lucinda said.

Nicole hurried along the corridor to meet her friends, Sheryl Ansel, Linda Barret and Angela Ellery. They were waiting for her by the lift.

"Come on, Nicole," Sheryl said. "You're late again. Have you been with Lucinda?"

"Yes. Where are we going?"

"To The Long Boat," Linda said. "John's giving us a lift."

They entered the lift, and Sheryl pressed the ground-floor button. Nicole smiled. All she could smell was Angela's perfume. She always went overboard with perfume. The four of them were very similar and could be taken as sisters. They were the same age, about the same height and had similar figures, except for Sheryl, who had a small bust. They had shoulder-length blonde hair and were pretty, although Sheryl was probably the prettiest. Sheryl never wore make-up, except for lipstick, and did not need to. Nicole felt undressed without makeup.

"I'm talking to you, Nicole," Angela said.

"I'm sorry. I was miles away."

They walked out of the lift.

"I said, is your date still on for tonight?" Angela asked.

"Yes. I'm meeting him outside the museum at eight."

"Has he got a car?" Sheryl asked. "And what's his name?"

"Brad. I don't think he's got a car."

"I wouldn't bother with him," Linda said. "I hate using the bus on dates. What you need is a rich man with a flashy car."

"Is Brad handsome?" Angela asked.

"Yes. Very."

They walked out of the building and into the car park.

"Come on, you lot," John, who was sitting in his car, shouted through the car window. "I've been waiting for fifteen minutes."

"Stop moaning, John," Sheryl said.

They climbed into John's car. Nicole sat between Linda and Sheryl, and Angela sat next to John.

"Is Brad tall?" Linda asked.

"Yes. He's over six feet tall."

"Are you going to do it with him tonight?" Sheryl asked.

"No. I never do it on the first date."

Nicole's friends thought that she was an experienced nineteen-year-old. She had been out with three single men and two married men (she had not realised at the time that they were married), but she was far from experienced and was still a virgin. She would have to love a man and believe that she could spend the rest of her life with him before she would even consider having sex with him.

It had nearly happened with Tom. If she had not seen him with his wife and two daughters, she would have slept with him. He did not look old enough to have two daughters. She was now much more wary of men. The first thing she would do, if she decided that she liked Brad enough to have sex with him, was to visit his family and speak to his mother. Only then would she believe that he was not married. Men were such good liars.

*

Brad felt on top of the world. He had a date with Nicole and was meeting her at eight. There was nothing like a date with a beautiful woman to lift a man's spirits. To pass the time, he was hoping to have a game of snooker, that is, if one of his mates, Wayne, Dan or Carl, was at the snooker hall. Carl had started a new job and was unlikely to be there, and Wayne was hopeless at snooker, so he was hoping to meet up with Dan.

He leapt from the bus and ran to the snooker hall, which served as his second home. The building was in Ladywood, Birmingham and was so old and dilapidated, it was probably listed. Dan Carter was leaning against a wall outside the snooker hall. He was twenty-two, short, stocky, had a squashed-up face and a laugh that sounded like a distraught hyena.

"I was hoping I would find you here," Brad said.

"I've already got our name down," Dan said. "We'll be on in a few minutes. They've only got the pink and the black left. Where have you been?"

"To sign on."

"Have you got a fag?" Dan asked.

"Yes, but I've only got one packet. I'm taking a girl out tonight, and I was hoping to make them last."

Dan held out his hand. "Don't be so fucking mean. I'll pay for the table if you supply the fags. What girl?"

Brad offered Dan a cigarette and took one himself. There were now only fifteen cigarettes left. "Her name's Nicole." He lit both cigarettes. "She's a cracker."

Dan blew a cloud of smoke into the air. "You say that about every girl you take out."

"This time, I mean it. She's beautiful, and she's clever. She goes to Aston University. She was carrying a violin case, so I think she plays the violin. She might be a female Nigel ... what's his name?"

"Who?"

"That famous violinist. The chap with the scruffy hairstyle,"

"Fucked if I know."

"Kennedy. That's it. Nigel Kennedy."

"I thought he was an American president," Dan said. "What are Nicole's tits like? They're the two most important bits about a woman."

"Did I ever tell you that you have a dirty mind?" Brad said.

"Yes, loads of times. If I know you, she'll have massive tits. You've always been tit mad."

"Me," Brad said. He smiled. "I hadn't noticed her tits."

"You lying son of a bitch," Dan said. "They're the first thing you look at. Come on. We're on now."

They walked into the snooker hall, and Brad chalked his cue while Dan set up the table. "I've only met her once for about ten minutes, but I really took to her. I can see myself staying with her for longer than my usual month."

"I doubt it," Dan said. "She'll only have to mention marriage, and you'll be off."

"Hold on," Wayne Dexter shouted as he walked towards them with Carl Ward in tow. "We can make it a foursome. Me and Carl will take you on." He took off his coat. He was twenty-two, tall, slim, ugly and had a pointed chin.

Dan flicked a coin. "Call?"

"Heads," Wayne said. It was tails.

"Our break," Dan said. "I'll take it."

"I thought you were starting a new job today, Carl?" Brad asked.

"I did. I only lasted an hour." He was twenty-two, tall, muscular, average-looking, and had only a few functioning brain cells. "It was packing bacon and sausages in a freezing cold room. It would send me mad being in there all day."

"I've told him he can work for me," Wayne said. "A cool two hundred pounds a week tax-free for just a few hours' work. Money for old rope."

"I don't mind taking drugs, but I'm not supplying them," Carl said. "I want to stay out of prison."

Wayne took his shot and missed. "Fuck it. And the black is right over the hole." He looked at Carl. "Suit yourself, but if you want a car like mine and a wad like this ..." He took out a wad of twenty-pound notes. "... it's there for the taking."

Carl blew out his cheeks. "I'm sick of being skint. What do I have to do?"

"I'll tell you later," Wayne said.

Brad sank the red and the black but missed the next red. He leaned on his cue and looked at Wayne. "And before you ask me, the answer's no."

"I've no intention of asking you," Wayne said. "I know how you feel about drugs. Are you still going out with ... what's her name ... Sharon? The one with the big tits."

"No. She began to get on my nerves."

Carl missed his shot and walked over to Wayne. "What protection will I get if someone causes trouble?"

"None from the police. You'll only be carrying a small amount at a time. But if someone threatens you, I have minders to sort them out. Two black blokes."

"Are they as tasty as Brad?" Carl asked.

Wayne looked at Brad. "They're bigger than Brad but not as tasty. I've never met anyone as tasty as our Brad."

Brad smiled. "Anyone would think I was a violent person."

"Are you two playing?" Dan asked. "It's your turn, Wayne, and I've left the red over the fucking pocket."

Brad and Dan lost due to Carl playing out of his socks. At five o'clock, Brad walked home to get ready for his date. His house was at the back of the snooker hall, but to get there, he had to climb over a high fence; otherwise, it was a fifteen-minute walk. He walked into his house. His mother, Carol, was in the kitchen, washing up. "You live in the kitchen," he said.

"Oh, it's you," she said. "Did you sign on?"

"Yes."

His mother was forty-eight, plain-looking, had dyed black hair and was putting on weight. Even though she needed glasses for reading, she refused to wear them and was always squinting. She did not look much, but she had a heart of gold, and he loved her to bits.

She scrutinised him for a few seconds. "You haven't had a shave. Tim was looking for you. I think he's decided to go to college after all. He's finally agreed that an art A-level is a waste of time ..."

Brad had been telling his brother that for years.

"... and I think he's going to do computers."

"I'm going to have a shower," he said. "I've got a date."

"It's broken," she said. "See if you can fix it. Do you have a new girlfriend?"

"Broken," he said. "Cowing hell. I suppose I can have a look at it. Yes. Her name's Nicole."

"Why is it I never see any of your girlfriends?" she asked. "You never bring them home. Are you ashamed of us?"

"No." He was. The house was a dump, and his father could be a right awkward bugger at times. "I don't go out with them long enough."

Tim walked in. He was nineteen, six feet tall, slim and handsome. He was a big softy and hated violence as much as Brad loved it, or so their mother claimed. "Get your boots, Brad. There's a game on in the park."

"I haven't got time. I've got a date."

"Do I know her?" Tim asked.

"No," Brad said.

Brad's mother hung up the tea towel. "Dinner's nearly ready."

"I'll warm it up later," Tim said.

"You can't," she said. "The microwave's broke."

"Everything's broken around here," Tim moaned.

Brad walked upstairs to have a look at the shower. For thirty minutes, he tried to fix the shower. He eventually gave up. It did not matter what he did; he could not get it to work properly. The water came out fine, but it kept changing from freezing cold to boiling hot. He had to settle for a strip wash.

Chapter Three

It was just after eight o'clock on Friday evening. Nicole was in the centre of Birmingham, walking towards the museum entrance, where she had arranged to meet Brad. For some reason, she was a bundle of nerves. She had only known him for a few minutes and knew very little about him; nevertheless, she was hoping he liked her enough to turn up. He was very handsome and could probably pick and choose when it came to women.

She smiled as she remembered how they met. She should not have agreed to go for a drink with him, but she had found it difficult to resist his charms. He was handsome, funny and was ...

"Boo," Brad said as he jumped from behind the Iron Man statue. He had been watching her walk across the square. She had a very sexy walk.

She smiled. "You made me jump."

"I'm glad you turned up." He held her hand. "Come on. I know just the place to go for a drink. It's classy." He glanced at her. "Just right for a classy chick. The prices are reasonable, so we might just be able to afford two drinks. I hope you've eaten. If not, the best I can offer is a packet of crisps."

"I want to make something clear from the start," she said. "If you're hoping to jump into bed with me, you're going to be disappointed. I don't sleep around."

"I'm glad. It shows that my judgment of you was right." He stopped. "This is the place. What do you think?"

It was a public house by the reference library. "It seems like a nice place."

"What do you want for a drink?" he asked.

"Half a lager, please."

He bought a pint and a half of lager, and they sat down at a table outside the public house. He caught a whiff of her perfume, and it sent his pulse dancing. He offered her a cigarette. She took one. The more he saw of Nicole, the more he liked her. He lit both cigarettes.

"I'm trying to give them up," she said.

"Me too." He pulled on his cigarette and leaned back in his chair. "I'm a bugger for procrastinating. Why is it that such a good-looking woman like you hasn't got a boyfriend?"

"There's more to life than boyfriends. If you must know, I'm in between boyfriends at the moment."

He leaned on the table and grinned at her. "Would you like me to be your boyfriend?"

"I'll think about it. The last two men I went out with turned out to be married, which is why I now insist on meeting the mother of any man intending to take me out for a second time."

He frowned. "Are you serious?"

"Deadly."

He sipped his drink. "I am hoping to see you again, so I'll have to forget all the stories I intended to spin. I was going to tell you that I was a pilot and lived in a penthouse suite."

She was pleased that he wanted to see her again. He was growing on her. "Where do you live?"

"In Ladywood. Where do you live?"

"In Birchfield."

They sat in silence for a while.

"Are you serious about seeing my mother?" he asked.

She nodded.

He sighed. "Then I suppose I'll have to take you to see her. Don't expect much. We live in an old Victorian house that's falling to bits. We're a very poor family." She probably had rich parents and lived in a posh house. She would now make some excuse not to see him again.

"What are you doing with your life?" she asked. "Are you working?" She felt very relaxed in his company.

"No. I dropped out of college. I was studying science and maths. I had visions of going into forensics." He emptied his glass. "Science and especially maths began to drive me mad. I'm thinking of going back to college in September to do an A-level in business studies and then go to university."

"I think you should," she said. "A degree in anything is better than no degree." She remembered him saying that he was short of money. "Do you mind getting the drinks?" She placed a ten-pound note on the table. "I don't like going to the bar. I'm a feminist in some ways and very old-fashioned in others."

"I'd like to be able to throw my money about, but I haven't got any to throw about." He picked up the ten-pound note. "Same again?"

"Yes, please."

He could not quite make up his mind about Nicole. She would not be going out with him if she wanted a rich boyfriend. Not having a car was a dead giveaway. If she still went out with him after she had seen where he lived, his first impression of her would have been right.

Nicole could tell that he was not a scrounger. He had reluctantly taken her money and so must be broke. What he was like as a person was more important to her than how much money he had.

He bought the drinks, placed them on the table and sat down. "I don't like being broke. If I'm going to go out with you on a regular basis, I'll take this job I've been offered. It's a security job at the gas. The money's all right; it's the shifts I don't like. I hate working nights."

She sipped her drink. "I haven't said I will go out with you again."

"And I haven't said I'll take the job." He offered her a cigarette. She refused. "I was thinking out loud. I haven't decided whether to take you out again. It all depends on whether my mum likes you, and she can be very selective about the women I take out, especially the gold diggers."

"I don't see any gold," she said. "I will go out with you again. Are you going to introduce me to your mother?"

"I suppose so. We'll go after we've finished this drink."

"Do you have any brothers and sisters?" she asked.

"Yes. A brother. He's nineteen. Do you?"

"No. I'm an only child."

They sat in silence for a while and watched the antics of four drunken young men larking about.

If she were honest about her feelings, Brad affected her in a way no man had affected her before. He was not only a handsome man with an athletic physique, but also had a presence. He exuded masculinity, and she felt very secure and relaxed in his company. She had never been totally relaxed in Tom's company.

Twenty minutes later, after chatting about their favourite groups and pop stars, they caught the bus to Ladywood. He felt embarrassed about not having a car. He had passed his test, but the lessons had taken all of his savings, and he now had no money to buy a car. "I bet you usually go out with men who have cars?"

"Yes, but it wasn't the reason I went out with them. I don't mind travelling on the bus." She did. She would rather travel in a car, but she did not want to upset him.

The sight of his house made him cringe. It looked worse than he had realised. He had never looked at it properly before. The outside needed painting, and there were two broken windows. "This is it," he said. "I must warn you that it's not much better inside. My dad hates decorating, and so does my brother, Tim. I decorated the lounge, but then the money ran out."

"Not everyone can be rich," she said.

No, but I wish I was, he thought.

She followed him into the house. The hall was clean, although it did need decorating. A woman aged about fifty walked out of the lounge. She was small and friendly-looking.

"This is my mother," Brad said. "This is Nicole."

His mother looked surprised. "I don't believe it." She smiled at Nicole. "You're the first girlfriend of Brad's I've ever seen. My name's Carol."

"I'm pleased to meet you, Carol," Nicole said.

"Go on in and sit down," Carol said. "Would you like a cup of tea?"

"Yes, please," Nicole said.

Brad and Nicole walked into the lounge. He was relieved to see that his dad was not in. Tim was sitting on his own, watching television. "Tim, this is Nicole."

Tim looked surprised. "Good God. This is a first. Hello, Nicole."

"Hello, Tim," Nicole said.

Brad and Nicole sat down.

"I'm watching Aston Villa play in the European Cup," Tim said. "Do you like football, Nicole?"

"Not really. The only sport I like is tennis."

"I play tennis," Tim said. "I'll have to give you a game sometime."

"It's not tennis that you play, Tim," Brad said, without taking his eyes from the television screen. "What you play is an oversized version of ping pong."

"I can beat you anyway," Tim said.

"Anyone can beat me."

Brad's mother walked in carrying a tea tray containing four cups, a sugar bowl, a milk jug and a plate of biscuits. "I'm using my best cups, so don't chip them." She placed the tea tray on the coffee table and smiled at Nicole. "I was talking to my sons. I can tell that you have manners."

"What do you do, Nicole?" Tim asked as he helped himself to a biscuit.

"I'm at Aston University doing a degree in media studies. What do you do?"

"I'm doing an A-level in computer studies."

"I think Brad's thinking of going back to college," Carol said. "He's very clever. He just doesn't try."

"I didn't try because I wasn't sure what I wanted to do," Brad said. "I do now. I've decided to go back to college and do an A-level in business studies and an A-level in computer studies."

Carol sat down and picked up a cup of tea. "Help yourself to milk and sugar, Nicole."

While Brad and Tim watched the television, shouting at the referee and screaming when they scored, Nicole drank her tea and chatted to Carol. It was obvious that she thought the world of her sons, although she did not expect them to go to university. She did not think they had the stamina to stay the course.

Brad glanced at Nicole as she talked to his mother. They seemed to be getting on fine.

Nicole liked Brad's mother and Tim, and as strange as it would seem to some people, she would rather marry into an honest family like this than into a rich, false family. She hated false people.

When the football finished, Brad walked Nicole to the bus stop. He expected Nicole to have been put off by his family and where he lived, and he was reluctant to ask her out again, but what had he got to lose? She could only say no. "Do you intend to go out with me again?" he asked.

"Yes. When?"

He was shocked. "Er ... How about next Saturday?"

"Okay. I'll meet you outside the Pavilion at eight."

The bus came, and before he had time to kiss her, she had climbed on board. Fuck it. He had been looking forward to a kiss.

She was pleased that he had not tried to kiss her. She did not want to rush their relationship. She sat down by the window and waved to him. He smiled and waved back. He was very handsome, and she was looking forward to kissing him. You can tell so much from a kiss.

Brad walked home, smoking. Nicole seemed very nice. She was not just nice; she was also very attractive. He was looking forward to Saturday so that he could kiss her delicious lips and get his hands on her sexy body, although he did not expect her to jump into bed with him. He had the feeling that she would only have sex with someone she was in love with. He hoped so. It would be nice to go out with a decent woman for a change. Most of the women he went out with could not get their knickers off quickly enough. Some did not even bother to wear them. He wanted a decent girlfriend, someone he could trust. He was sick of one-night stands with tarts. He had a good feeling about Nicole.

Chapter Four

Nicole was in the lounge of her house. She checked her makeup in the mirror. It was ten past eight in the morning, and time for her to go to college. She looked out of the window. It was an overcast day, but at least it was not raining. Wind and rain played havoc with a girl's looks.

"When are we going to see this boyfriend of yours?" her father asked.

He was a loving father, but had a tendency to moan. It was about time her parents met Brad. "Today, if you like. I can phone him at work and ask him to come here."

"I'd love to meet him," her mother said. She had changed her appearance. She had dyed her hair and was now wearing contact lenses. She looked ten years younger. "Is he taking you to the party?"

"Yes. It's at Angela's house in Sutton Coldfield."

Her father frowned. "I hope he doesn't turn out to be married."

"He's not married. I've been to his house several times. His mother's very nice. I think you would like her. His brother Tim is easy to get on with, but his father seems to be a moody person." She almost added, just like you are sometimes.

"What time will he be here?" her father asked. "I don't want to miss him."

"About eight o'clock. He's working till six. I'll have to go, or I'll miss the bus."

*

At lunchtime in the Aston University canteen, Nicole took Angela to one side. "Can we stop the night at your house, Angela?"

"You and Brad?"

"Yes."

"I suppose you want a bedroom?"

"If possible."

"It'll have to be the small spare bedroom we use to store things in. The other four bedrooms are spoken for."

"It'll do just fine," Nicole said.

Angela smiled and nudged her arm. "I know what you'll be doing tonight."

"Mind your own business," Nicole said.

"I don't know why you have to be so secretive," Angela said. "I tell you all about my love life."

"I just don't like to talk about things like that, and if I found out that Brad talked about our sex life, I would finish with him."

"He doesn't. I asked him."

Nicole was shocked. "You didn't?"

"I did. I asked him last week."

“What did he say?”

“He said, and I quote, I never talk about sex; I just do it.” Angela sighed. “He’s all man. I wish he would do me.”

“You are disgusting, Angela.”

Nicole was pleased that Brad did not talk about their sex life. Not that there had been anything to talk about, although there would be by tomorrow if all went as planned. She just hoped that Brad would not be able to tell that she was a virgin.

*

Brad ran from his place of work and jumped straight on the bus, which was a bit fortuitous. He sat down and frowned. He was not looking forward to meeting Nicole’s parents. It made it look as if he was serious about Nicole. He liked her, but he had no intention of getting married or even engaged. They had not even had sex yet, and until they did, they were not an item. Each time they met, he would drop into the conversation that he would like to have sex with her, and she would say something like, I’m not the sort to jump into bed with a man. He had never desired a woman more, and would have to have a serious discussion with her to find out when they would be having sex.

As he walked from the bus to his house, he met up with Wayne and Carl.

“I made three hundred pounds tax-free last week,” Carl boasted.

“Just make sure you stay out of prison,” Brad said.

“I’m branching out,” Wayne said. “I’m supplying all over the place now. I’m what they call a middleman. The offer of a job is still open, Brad. It’s better than security.”

“Most things are better than security,” Brad said as he walked into his road. “See you around.”

It only took him fifty-five minutes to have his meal, get washed and changed and get to Nicole’s house. It made a change to have some decent clothes to wear and some money in his pocket. He knocked on Nicole’s door. She lived in a house very similar to his, except that the exterior was nicely decorated, and it was in a slightly better area. He was hoping that her parents were as easy to get on with as Nicole was.

*

“It’s the door,” Nicole’s father shouted.

“I’ll get it,” Nicole said. She walked into the hall and opened the front door. It was Brad. He looked very smart. “Come in.”

He stepped inside the house. “You look devastatingly beautiful.”

“Thanks.” She guided him into the lounge where her parents were waiting. “This is Brad. These are my parents.”

“Hi, folks,” Brad said.

“Pleased to meet you,” Nicole’s father said as he shook hands with Brad. “I’m Andy.”

Brad smiled. Nicole's father seemed amicable enough. At a guess, he would say he was more bark than bite. Nicole's mother was the spitting image of a teacher he had at school.

"I'm Pat," Nicole's mother said. "Take a seat, Brad."

"We're not stopping," Nicole said. "Otherwise, we'll be late." She slipped on her coat. "I'll see you tomorrow." She pushed Brad out of the room.

"It was nice meeting you, even though it was brief," Nicole's mother said.

"Bye," Brad shouted from the hall.

They stepped outside, and Nicole closed the door behind them. "If we had sat down, we would have been there for hours."

"I wouldn't have minded," he said. "They're not what I expected. They seem easy enough to get on with."

"They are," she said.

Nicole's house was spick and span and contained decent furniture. By comparison, it made his house look like a right dump. "Is that our bus?"

"Yes."

He took her hand, and they ran down the road. The bus driver saw them and stopped the bus.

The journey to Sutton Coldfield took them from the overcrowded, impoverished part of Birmingham through a slightly better part of suburbia and then to the abode of the bourgeoisie. Most of the houses in this area were detached, had a double garage and large, well-kept gardens. They climbed off the bus, crossed a road and walked up the drive of a large detached house with a double garage and several hundred-foot-tall fir trees in the front garden.

"I wouldn't mind living here," he said.

"It's a dream house," she said as she rang the bell.

Angela opened the door. "Come on in and help yourselves to food and drink. We don't charge."

A few minutes later, he was left to his own devices while Nicole and Angela went to powder their noses. He sat smoking and drinking. Music was playing, and the few people present were talking quietly in small groups. He could sense an uneasy atmosphere. It was the saddest party he had ever been to. Perhaps someone had died.

Nicole returned and sat down next to him. "Sheryl's fallen out with Linda," she whispered. "They're not talking."

"Why have they fallen out?"

"They've had a disagreement over a man. I tried to talk to Sheryl, but it didn't do any good. Sheryl swears she'll never talk to Linda again."

"It looks to have put the kibosh on the party," he said. "I've been to happier wakes."

Linda sat down next to Nicole. "Did you have a word with Sheryl?"

Nicole nodded. "It didn't do any good."

Linda sipped her drink. "I didn't know that Sheryl was keen on Richard. She never told me. And all I did was have a snog with him."

"Did you let him feel your tits?" Nicole asked.

"Yes, but it's no big deal. I've now told Richard to piss off, and I wouldn't have snogged with him if I'd known that he was taking Sheryl out next week. It's Richard's fault. If Sheryl had any sense, she would dump him."

Brad was keeping well out of it. From what he could tell, both Sheryl and Linda were birdbrains. He sipped his drink and admired the furniture and fittings. It would be grand to live in such a large, beautiful house. At a guess, he would say that it was worth at least eight hundred thousand pounds. The price would keep such houses well out of his reach. That is, unless he went to university and got a degree. He might then just be able to reach.

Linda walked off, and Nicole shook her head. "I've given up trying to sort them out. I don't want them to spoil our special night."

He frowned. "Why is it a special night?"

"We've been going out with each other for over a month, and we still like each other."

He smiled. "I like you a lot."

She stared at him. "How much?"

He blew out his cheeks. "What a question." He sipped his drink. "Quite a lot, if I'm honest." He was not being completely honest. He liked her more than he was willing to admit.

"I also like you a lot," she said. "We also get on very well, and we don't argue."

"We seem to have clicked," he said. "I feel relaxed with you, and I don't feel I have to prove myself, although I'd like to get more than a goodnight kiss and a feel."

"I don't like to rush relationships," she said.

He squeezed her hand. "As long as you know that I fancy you rotten and that I want to make love to you."

"Would tonight be soon enough?" she asked.

He nearly dropped his drink. "What did you say?"

She smiled. "I've booked us a room."

"Where?"

"Here. It's the small bedroom."

At first, he thought she was joking, but now realised she was serious. "Great. I hope you don't go and change your mind. I want you more than you will ever know."

"Good, but you will have to wait. I intend to enjoy the party first."

He looked about. "For that to happen, it will have to liven up a bit."

Sheryl had a good cry and then made it up with Linda just before the stripogram arrived. He was a muscle-bound freak who did nothing for Nicole. An athletic male body turned her on, but not when it was covered in lumps of muscle. Angela loved muscle men, and she was all over the stripogram. She took several selfies with her arms around him.

The male stripogram left, and the female stripogram arrived. Nicole watched Brad. He was goggle-eyed until she took off her top. He then lost interest and leaned against the piano. This was not the Brad she had grown to understand and like. She walked over to him. "You can't see much from here."

"I'm not really bothered."

"Why? Doesn't she have a beautiful figure?"

"No. Not in my opinion."

Nicole had a good look at the half-naked stripper, who was all over Angela's boyfriend. As far as she could tell, the stripper had a perfect body: huge breasts, a pretty face and a slim figure. "I can't see anything wrong with her. Don't you like big breasts?"

"Yes. The bigger, the better, but they have to be real. They have to be natural. I hate the silicon lumps that many women now have. They turn me right off. They don't bounce, and if the woman lies down, they stick up in the air. Silicon-filled breasts are more like the breasts on a statue than flesh and blood. And look at her bum."

Nicole did and could not see anything wrong with it. "What's wrong with her bum?"

"It's too slim. It's like a man's bum. I bet she's had liposuction."

"How is it like a man's bum?" she asked.

"It's too small, and she has no lumps on her hips. It's the lumps that make the difference between a man and a woman. Viva la difference."

"Oh, I see." She was secretly pleased. She had large, floppy breasts and love handles. Up until now, she had despised her love handles. She was now beginning to like them. As long as Brad liked her figure, she would not mind being slightly overweight.

Brad watched Nicole walk across the room towards Angela. If he were any judge of women, he would say that Nicole had the figure he liked. He would soon find out. He could not wait. Up until tonight, he had not even had a proper feel of her tits. He had tried several times, but she had pulled his hands away. Women were very strange creatures. Why had she waited a month before agreeing to sleep with him? A week was more than long enough to know whether you fancy someone or not.

Nicole felt nervous about sleeping with Brad, and she was a little tipsy when she walked upstairs to the small bedroom with him later that evening. Most of the partygoers had retired to their bedrooms. Nicole had left it as late as possible. She was now only minutes away from discovering what sex was like. "I know you're a man of the world, but I would like to lay down a few ground rules."

They walked into the bedroom, and he closed the door. "What do you mean?"

"I only want to have sex in the missionary position, at first, anyway. I'm a little nervous."

"I don't mind." He suddenly realised that he did not have a condom. "Oh, sod it. I haven't got a Johnny."

"I have." She took the condom out of her handbag and placed it on the bed. She was just going to leave everything to him.

He took her in his arms, kissed her on the lips and felt her breasts. They were large and natural.

"Are they how you like them?" she asked.

"Yes. They're perfect."

They undressed down to their underwear and climbed onto the bed.

Even though she was tipsy, she was a bundle of nerves and did not expect to climax the first time. He began to caress her body and kiss her neck. It was nice to have her body touched. He took off her bra but left her pants on.

He had not expected her body to be so beautiful and to feel so soft and feminine. For a few minutes, he enjoyed the feel of her breasts and her backside. She still looked nervous, and her legs were pressed together. "Are you still feeling nervous?"

"Yes, but I'm beginning to relax."

"Is it your first time?" he asked.

"Yes."

"I thought it was, but there is nothing to be nervous about. Tell me when you want me to do it." He kissed her on the lips and began to rub her clitoris.

She ran her hands up and down his body, and the nervous tension began to drift away. She was now eager for him to enter her. "You can do it now."

About bloody time, he thought. He rolled on the condom and climbed up on top of her. He lifted up her legs and pushed his penis into her.

When he began to thrust into her, she sank into a world of sheer delight. A world she did not know existed. Her body seemed to melt and swish about as a powerful surge of pleasure overwhelmed her.

It had been some time since he had sex, and the thrill of her body was too much for him. He had intended for her to climax first, but he could not hold back anymore. He took a firm grip of her backside and thrust deep into her.

The intense pleasure carried her body in an upward spiral, and she hugged him as she climaxed. The pleasure was almost painful. "Oh. Oh. Oh. Ohhhhh."

The timing was perfect. He climaxed as she cried out, and his body shook. He could thank the lager for holding him back just long enough for her to climax. It had worked out perfectly.

For several minutes, she lay under him, hugging him. She did not want him to move. It had been very special, even more special and enjoyable than she had expected. Her friends were forever talking about how fantastic sex was. She now understood what they meant. It was amazing, and there was nothing to compare it to. But had Brad enjoyed it as much? "Did you enjoy it?"

"I'll say I did." He rolled off her and took off the condom. "It blew my mind. Was your first time special for you?"

"Yes. It was wonderful."

"Are we going to do this again?" he asked.

"Yes, if you want to."

"I want to. I'm falling asleep."

They lay down, and she pulled the duvet over them. He fell asleep, and she cuddled up to him. There was no mistaking how she felt. She was in love. It was such an overwhelming feeling. She was bursting with happiness and felt that they were now emotionally and physically entwined. He was perfect for her in every way and was the man of her dreams. Having sex and falling in love was a major happening in her life, although she intended to keep it to herself. She was not going to tell anybody, even her friends, and certainly not Brad. She wanted to get to know everything about him before she told him that she loved him, and that would only be after he had declared his love for her.

CHAPTER FIVE

It started raining as Nicole waited for her bus to take her to the university. She had forgotten the new umbrella she had bought. She pulled her hood over her head and stepped into an entry doorway, pressing her back against a gate. She was only partially protected from the lashing rain and would be soaked by the time the bus arrived, and when it did, there would probably be two of them. Buses always seemed to travel in twos.

The gate behind her opened, and she fell backwards. Someone grabbed her, spun her around and hit her in the stomach. The blow was powerful, and it doubled her up. She was winded and unable to speak. Her hands were quickly tied behind her back, and tape was put over her mouth and eyes. She could hardly breathe and tried to struggle. Someone hit her in the stomach again, and all the fight left her. She had been hit extremely hard, and the pain was unbearable.

She felt herself being lifted and carried and then bundled into what felt like a small cupboard. A car engine started up. The vibration told her that she was in the boot of a car. She felt confused and could not breathe properly. Why had she been kidnapped? She had no money, and neither did her family.

A short time later, she was taken out of the boot of the car, carried a short distance and thrown to the ground. The tape was removed from around her mouth, and she gasped for air. It took a few seconds for her mind to clear. She had nearly suffocated.

"I'm talking to you," someone was saying. "Can you hear me?"

"Yes." He sounded West Indian and smelled of curry and cigarettes.

"I'm going to untie you," he said. "If you cry out or try to take the tape off your eyes, I will kill you. Do you understand?"

"Yes." She was now very frightened. He sounded as if he would kill her.

He pulled her to her feet, took the tape from around her wrists and began to feel her breasts. "We've got ourselves a fit one here, John."

She had not realised there were two of them. "Please let me go. I'll ..." Someone punched her in the stomach. The pain was excruciating.

"If you say another word, I'll break your fucking arms," John said. His voice was gruff. He was also West Indian. "Phone George. He'll want to fuck her first."

Nicole was now terrified and on the verge of tears. She was about to be raped by at least three men. She also believed that she was going to be killed when they had finished with her. She had read about men raping women and then killing them.

"This is Toss, George. We've struck lucky this time. She's white, has big tits and a nice arse. No, we haven't touched her. Sure."

"What did George say?" John asked Toss.

"He sounded pleased. He's on his way."

"Where is he?" John asked.

"At The Old Mill. He should be here in five minutes."

Wherever she was being held, she was a five-minute car ride from The Old Mill. She wanted to remember everything so that she would be able to tell the police, although any amount of knowledge she amassed would be useless if they killed her.

One of the men began to squeeze her breasts. He then pulled up her dress and pushed his fingers into her vagina. It hurt, but she did not complain. She did not want to be hit again.

A few minutes later, John said, "It's George. I'd know the sound of his car anywhere."

She heard footsteps on a staircase and the sound of a door opening.

"What do you think, George?" Toss asked.

"Fucking perfect," George said. He was also West Indian. "Just how I like em. White with big tits." He had a very deep voice.

"I know how to pick em, George," Toss said.

Someone, she suspected it was George, grabbed hold of her and squeezed her breasts hard.

"Do what we tell you," George said. "If you don't, we'll cut your fucking face."

"I will," she said. She had never been so frightened in her life.

"Where are the Jonnies?" George asked.

"In this box," Toss said.

George turned her around, pushed her over what felt like a table and pulled up her dress. "Stick your arse out," he said.

She did as she was told. Perhaps when they had raped her, they would let her go. He began to thrust into her. She was dry, and it was painful. It seemed to go on forever.

"I fucking needed that," George said as he pulled his penis out of her. "When you've fucked her, get up to The Sack. We've got some business on."

She stood up and was pushed back over the table. "Don't fucking move until we tell you to," a man said. It was a voice she had not heard before. He was also a West Indian. "Stick your arse out. That's it."

She lay still as he thrust into her. They were very aggressive men, and it would be foolish and dangerous to aggravate them.

"Get a fucking move on, Sam," Toss said. "I'm fucking dying here."

"Stop fucking moaning," Sam said. "You can't rush a good fuck."

When Sam had finished, Toss and then John raped her from behind. The pain was unbearable. Each time they thrust into her, a hot blade of pain crashed through her body. She was terrified and began to cry silently.

"Yes," George said. He sounded as if he were speaking into a phone. "I fucking know. Yes. We're on our way."

She heard someone open a door. She did not move or pull her dress down.

"Make sure that she has food and water, Vic," George said. "She's got to last for a few months."

"I'll look after her," Vic said. He sounded a little frightened of George. "I always do."

She heard four men walk down the stairs. One of the stairs creaked each time it was stepped on. There was now only Vic in the room. She heard the door being shut.

"Now for a bit of fucking fun," Vic said.

He pushed something into her vagina. It hurt, and she cried out.

"Shut your fucking trap," he said. "Nothing turns me on like a tart with a bottle up her cunt. Stick your arse out. That's it."

"That's a good one," he said. "I'll add these to my collection."

She suddenly realised that he was taking pictures of her.

He pulled the bottle out and pushed his hand up inside her vagina. The pain was excruciating, and she only just managed to suppress a scream. She pressed her teeth together and remained silent. It felt as if he was trying to tear out her insides.

"You whites are all the fucking same," he said. He pulled her hair. "Stand up. Bounce your tits up and down."

She stood up and bounced her breasts up and down. She suspected he was taking more pictures of her. There were now two little pools of tears under the tape over her eyes. He pushed her onto what felt like a bed.

"Lie down," he said.

She lay down, and he pushed his penis into her mouth. It smelled vile and tasted disgusting, and she was nearly sick.

"Suck me off," he said. "And if you bite me, I'll cut your face off. Move your fucking tongue about. That's it. Ohh, fucking lovely." He began to squeeze her breasts hard as if he were trying to rip them off her chest. She was now floating in a sea of pain.

"When I come, swallow it," he said. "If you spit it out, I'll break your fucking legs."

He squeezed her breasts even harder as he climaxed. She felt the sperm pump into her mouth. She tried not to swallow.

"Fucking swallow it," he shouted.

He squeezed her breasts so hard she was forced to swallow the sperm so that she could cry out. It was the worst pain she had ever felt.

"That'll teach you, you fucking bitch," he said.

Her thoughts were now hazy and mixed up. She had a feeling that she had passed out. The room was quiet, except for Vic's intermittent swearing and a beeping sound. He was obviously playing a video game of some sort.

She considered asking Vic to let her go, but decided against it. He would probably hurt her. She had to do something, but what? From what Sam had said, they intended to keep her here for months. How could she possibly endure being tied up and raped for months? She would rather die.

She heard a distant tapping sound. Vic stood up, left the room and ran downstairs. She could hear distant voices. A few seconds later, Vic walked back up the stairs.

"Sit up," Vic said. "I've got some sandwiches and a bottle of pop. You're going to eat them, or I'll shove them down your throat. Sit up."

She sat up and drank most of the pop. She was very thirsty. She then tried to eat the sandwiches. A draught of fresh air fanned her face when a window was opened. She could hear distant traffic.

Time seemed to stand still. She needed to go to the toilet, but she was too afraid to ask.

Vic left the room. A short time later, a chain was pulled, and Vic walked back into the room. "Do you want a piss?" he asked.

She nodded.

He took her arm and pulled her to her feet. He was very strong. He led her out of the room and into a toilet. It smelled of urine and excrement. She sat down on the seat. It was wet. She relieved herself and was led back to the room.

"Lie down and don't fucking move," he said.

She lay down. They were animals and would probably kill her when they had finished with her, and so she must try to escape, but how? She was being watched and was too frightened to remove the tape that was over her eyes. She cried silently as he played his video game.

Chapter Six

Brad was cheesed off with his security job. Twelve-hour shifts were a killer. He was now on a rota of six days and then six nights with three days off in between. He would only be able to see Nicole on his three days off. On nights, he tried to do a bit of studying to help pass the time. Tried was the operative word. His partner, Dave Hunt, talked almost non-stop. Days involved more work, and so did not drag as much as nights. It was seven-thirty in the morning, and he had just started his day shift. He stood by the window, watching the gate as the factory workers came into work.

"The fucking cheeky sod," Brad said.

Dave, who was sitting down reading, looked up. "What's the matter?" Dave was thirty-seven, small, thin and ugly.

"The woman whose car I searched yesterday has just driven past and given me a filthy look," Brad said. "Just wait until she tries to leave. I'll search her car every day for the rest of the fucking week."

Dave smiled. "I thought you liked women."

"I do, but only when they're bending over," Brad said.

"I'll tell Nicole what you said when I see her."

"You'd better not. She's a decent woman. Anyway, she'd never talk to the likes of you." He turned around. "Are you smoking?"

"Yes. Do you want a drag?"

"Yes. You'll get us sacked for smoking on duty." Brad took the cigarette, had a drag and handed it back. "It's going to be a long day."

"It always fucking is," Dave said.

Brad was already missing Nicole. He had only known her for a few weeks, but now thought the world of her.

*

Nicole woke up as someone shook her.

"Lie on your back," George said. "It's fun time again."

She turned onto her back. Her vagina was sore, her insides hurt, and her breasts were bruised. There was no way she would be able to survive for months being treated like a blow-up doll.

"Pull your dress right up and open your legs," George said.

She did as she was told. Her hands touched her breasts as she pulled up her dress, and she almost cried out. They felt extremely bruised.

"What the fuck's happened here?" George said.

"What?" Vic asked. "What's wrong?"

"Look at her tits," George said. There was a thump and then a crash as if someone had fallen over.

"For fuck sake, don't hit me again, George," Vic said. "You don't know your own strength. I just squeezed a bit hard."

"What have I told you about damaging my merchandise?" George said. "Her fucking tits are covered in bruises. They don't even look like fucking tits."

"She must bruise easy," Vic said. "I think you've broken my jaw."

"I'll break your fucking neck if you damage my property again," George said.

"I won't, George, honest," Vic said.

Even though her breasts were bruised, it did not prevent them from squeezing them as they raped her. She cried out each time they squeezed her breasts. She could hear them laughing. After all five men had raped her, she lay on the bed crying. She was in agony. How could men be so cruel? If they wanted sex, there were plenty of women willing to provide it.

The door opened, and the men began to leave. "Keep her tied up," George said.

"I will," Vic said.

She counted four sets of footsteps as the men walked down the stairs. Vic was now the only one left in the room. He had already raped her, and so he might leave her alone.

"The fucking bastard," he said. "I hope someone cuts his fucking throat." He was talking to himself. He walked out of the room. "What's the number of our dentist?"

He was speaking on the phone, and she could just hear what he was saying.

"I don't fucking know," he said. "Look in the book. I've got a fucking pen. Just tell me the number. Yes. I'll see you on Friday."

She curled up into a ball on the bed. Her whole body was wracked with pain. There was only so much she could take. She would have to get away.

Vic began to walk downstairs. "Is that the dentist? Yes. I usually see Mr Price. It's an emergency. Yes. I have two loose teeth. I need ..."

She could no longer hear what he was saying. She hoped that he was in pain. If she were a man, she would knock out more of his teeth.

A short time later, he walked back upstairs and into the room. He seemed to be searching for something. "Fuck it," he said. He taped up her mouth and tied her arms and legs together. "If you move, I'll hear you. And if you try to remove the tape over your eyes, I will know."

He walked out of the room, used the toilet without pulling the chain, and walked downstairs. She did not hear a door shutting, but she sensed that he had left the building. He was probably going to the dentist.

The tape over her mouth was preventing her from breathing, and she began to panic. She was in an awkward position. Her legs were tied to the bottom of the bed, and her arms were tied to the top. She rubbed her face against the bed and managed to remove some of the tape that was over her mouth. She was now able to breathe properly. She then realised that her left hand was not taped up very tightly. He must have run out of tape.

She pulled hard on the tape, and her left hand came free. She took the tape off her eyes. The room was filthy, and part of the ceiling had fallen in. It was probably a derelict house. If they came back now and saw that she had removed the tape from over her eyes, they would probably break her legs or cut her face, and so she must get away.

As much as she tried, she could not get the tape off her right wrist. She had pulled it into the shape of a rope and so could not peel it off layer by layer, and it was too strong to break. She could not reach the tape with her teeth, and could not reach the tape around her ankles that tied her to the bottom of the bed. She was near to tears. She had to get away, but she was tied up too securely.

The bed she was lying on was old, and the headboard looked rotten. It looked to be the bottom half of a bunk bed. She began to kick the wood at the bottom of the bed. Something broke. She kicked harder, and the rail came off. She was now able to move up the bed a little and reach the tape around her wrist with her teeth. The tape was very difficult to bite through, and it was taking ages. If she did not hurry, Vic could return. Minutes stretched into what seemed like an hour. She began to cry. The tape would not come off. If only she had not pulled it into a rope.

She then noticed a knife on a small table. If only she could reach the knife. She lifted her feet, which were taped to the broken rail and manoeuvred her body so that she was sitting on the side of the bed. She might be able to drag the table to within reach. She tried several times, but the rail that was tied to her feet prevented her pulling the table towards her. It was useless, and she began to sob. They would do terrible things to her for trying to escape.

She was such a fool. She should have realised. The table was on a rug. She carefully pulled the rug towards her with her feet and brought the table within reach. She picked up the knife and cut through the tape on her wrists and ankles. It took just a few seconds.

She stood up and listened. All she could hear was the sound of distant traffic. She walked over to the door. Her legs were weak. She tried to open the door. Oh, no. It was locked. She had not heard him lock the door. She walked over to the window. It overlooked a long garden. There was a flat roof below the window, and she should be able to climb onto it. It was corrugated, but it looked strong enough to support her weight.

She opened the window and climbed out onto the roof. It felt solid, and as long as she kept to where the nails attached the corrugated sheets to the beams, she should be all right. She walked slowly across the roof. It was slanted and difficult to walk on.

The roof gave way with an almighty crash, and she fell through to the floor below. She landed on her side and bumped her head. She felt dazed. She stood up and tried to sort her thoughts out. She had to get away. The door to the building she had fallen into, which looked like a shed, was open, and she walked out into an overgrown garden. It took all of her strength to walk the full length of the garden, climb through a gap in the fence and walk to the main road. She then collapsed. She was totally exhausted. For a while, she felt herself slipping in and out of consciousness.

The face of a black man appeared in front of her, and she feared that he was one of the men who had raped her. He was saying something to her. "Please don't hurt me," she said.

"I'm not going to hurt you," he said. "Can I help you?"

He had a kind face and did not have the voice of one of the rapists. She sat up. She was now frightened of all black men, but some must be good. "Are you a good man?" she asked.

He nodded. He was about sixty and had a wrinkled face and grey hair. "Are you ill?" he asked.

"Will you please help me to get to 57 Hurbert Road in Birchfield? My parents will pay for the taxi."

"Yes, of course." He took her arm. "I know Hurbert Road."

She lost consciousness, and his face drifted away.

*

Brad walked out of his security office. It was situated near the gate of the factory. He walked up to the car belonging to the woman who had given him a dirty look for searching her car. "Could you open your boot, please, madam?" he said.

"I will not," she said through the open car window. She was good-looking in a tarty sort of way. She also looked to have a vile temper.

"Then you will not be leaving the premises with your car," he said.

"We will see about that," she said. She picked up her mobile phone and pressed in some numbers. "A security guard will not let me out of the gates," she said into the phone. "Get down here and sort him out."

A car pulled up behind the woman's car, and the driver leaned out of the window. "What's going on?" he asked.

"I'm searching this lady's car," Brad said. "I'll be as quick as I can."

"You will not be searching this car," she said.

Brad bent down and looked in the car window. "Do you want to bet? I'll give you odds of ten to one."

"You cheeky bastard," she said.

A few minutes later, the managing director walked towards them. "What is the problem, young man?" he asked Brad.

"He won't let me go through the gates," the woman said.

"Let me sort it out, Gloria," the managing director said. He turned to Brad. "Let the lady through; there's a good man."

"No," Brad said. "Not until I've searched her car."

The managing director looked shocked. "Do you realise who I am?" he asked.

"Yes," Brad said.

Several cars behind the woman's car began to sound their horns.

"Let him search your car, Gloria," the managing director said. "I'll make sure that he doesn't bother you again."

Gloria climbed out of her car. She looked angry enough to burst. "You'll be getting the sack for this," she seethed.

Brad did not care either way. He was sick of the job. He smiled at her. "Could you open the boot, please, madam?"

"It's not a laughing matter," she said as she opened the boot.

"I'm just being friendly," Brad said. It was all he could do to stop laughing out loud. He looked in the boot. It contained a large bag. "Could you open the bag?"

She opened the bag, and he looked in. It contained dozens of toilet rolls, probably stolen from the stores. "Have a look in the bag, Dave." Dave had a look in the bag and then stepped back without saying anything. "Thank you, madam," Brad said. "You can now close the boot and leave the premises."

She closed the boot and climbed into her car. As soon as the barrier was lifted, she drove off at breakneck speed. Brad burst out laughing. "That'll teach her."

"The managing director's listening," Dave whispered.

"Fuck him," Brad said. "I'm only doing my job." He waved the other cars through.

*

Nicole woke up to the sound of her mother's voice. "Nicole. Nicole. Speak to me, for God's sake."

Nicole opened her eyes. She was at home. She was in her front room on the settee and was safe. She sat up, threw her arms around her mother, hugged her and sobbed. It was only after Nicole had cried herself out that she was able to speak.

"Where have you been?" her mother asked. "You are filthy."

"I was kidnapped and raped."

Her mother looked shocked. "Oh my God."

"Can I have something to eat and drink?" Nicole asked.

"Yes. I'll phone your father.

Nicole had a shower, changed into clean clothes, and ate a meal her mother had prepared. After eating, she sat in the lounge with a cup of tea.

Her father walked into the room. He looked worried. "What happened? You didn't say on the phone."

"Nicole was kidnapped and raped," her mother said.

He looked upset. "Bleeding hell. Have you phoned the police?"

"No," her mother said. "I was waiting for you to come home."

"I'll phone them now."

A short time later, a policewoman arrived and took a statement. Nicole was now very tired. All she wanted to do was go to bed. A short time after the policewoman had left, a female doctor arrived and examined her. She took samples from inside her vagina to test for DNA and left.

Her mother handed Nicole a glass of water and two tablets. "Take these tablets. The doctor said they will help you relax."

It felt as if Nicole was living in a dream, a misty dream. She took the tablets, walked upstairs and crawled into bed. She was safe. She was no longer going to be raped and abused by evil savages.

*

The following afternoon, Brad once again stopped Gloria's car. She had stuck her fingers up at him on her way into work, and he was not going to stand for that. "Can I look into your boot, please?" Brad said.

"No, you cannot," she said through the car window.

The managing director, who had been watching, walked over to Brad. "Why are you harassing this woman?"

"It's a security matter and has nothing to do with you, sir," Brad said.

"Move your car over there, Gloria," the managing director said, and he pointed. "I'll phone the security manager. He'll sort it out."

She moved her car, and a short time later, Brad's supervisor, Garry, arrived. He was a stupid prat, and Brad had no time for him.

"What the fuck are you doing?" Garry asked.

"My job. What do you think I'm doing?"

"He's harassing this woman by continually searching her car," the managing director said.

"Let that woman's car through now," Garry said. "Peter will be here in a few minutes."

Brad expected to get the sack, so he decided to cause as much trouble as possible. "Piss off."

Garry just stood there with his mouth open.

A short time later, Peter, the owner of the security firm, arrived. Brad had always got on with him. Peter took Brad into the security hut. "What the bloody hell's going on?" Peter asked. "I've had the managing director on the phone to me. He wants you sacked."

"It's nothing I can't handle," Brad said. "Some bitch didn't want her car searched, and so she fetched the managing director, who told me not to search her car. I told him politely that I decide whose car I search, and if someone tries to stop me from searching their car, I'll make sure that it's searched. My job is to stop thieving from this factory, and if need be, I'll search the managing director's car."

Peter blew out his cheeks. "It's what I told you to do, and thieving has been reduced. Leave it to me."

Peter had a private word with Dave and then went outside to speak to the managing director, who was talking to Gloria. Brad opened the window so that he could hear what was being said.

"No, I will not be dismissing the security guard," Peter said. "He's just doing his job. When someone intimidates a security guard, it means that they have something to hide and need watching."

"So, he can search my car every day?" Gloria asked.

"Yes. If he so chooses," Peter said. He turned to the managing director. "He can also search your car."

"This is ridiculous," Gloria said. "Can I leave?"

"Yes," Peter said.

Dave opened the barrier, and she drove off.

"I assure you that Gloria's a very trustworthy person," the managing director said.

"Then why did she have a large bag full of dozens of toilet rolls in her boot?" Peter asked.

Brad smiled. Dave must have told Peter about the toilet rolls.

The managing director looked shocked. "Did she?"

"Yes. It'll be in my report," Peter said. "Because she's already been caught stealing, I'll expect my security guards to be extra vigilant."

Brad shut the window so they could not hear him laughing. The job was pants, but it had its good points.

Chapter Seven

Brad had finished the night shifts and now had three long days off. It was a huge relief to know that he could forget about work for a while. His job was driving him mad. As he walked home, he thought once again about working for Wayne. It would be risky, but it could be worth it. In a few months, he could save enough to get a decent motor and put a few quid in the bank. He then remembered what had happened to Kelly. No. Working for Wayne was not an option. He would have to stick it out where he was or get another job.

He walked down the path to his house and into the kitchen. He was starving, but all there was to eat in the house was one piece of stale bread. He pushed it into the toaster. Toasting might make it edible. It was typical. He was working all hours and paying cash to his mother for food, and there was sod all to eat.

The toaster exploded, and the toast shot into the air in a cloud of smoke. He caught the toast and put it quickly onto the worktop. It was too hot to hold. The toaster was on fire, so he switched it off at the plug. "Bleeding typical," he said.

He looked closely at the smouldering piece of toast. It had a dark stain on one corner and smelled of oil. Who the hell would put oil in a toaster?

Tim walked into the kitchen. "The house is full of smoke. What happened?"

"The toaster exploded."

"Oh, sod it," Tim said. "I only fixed it yesterday."

Brad rolled his eyes. "No bleeding wonder it exploded. Don't ever touch anything electrical again."

"I was only trying to help," Tim said.

"Your bleeding help nearly killed me," Brad said.

Brad was tired, but he was also starving, so he walked to a cafe to have breakfast. He already had most of his meals out. On the way back from the café, he stepped into the telephone box and phoned Nicole's number. He felt lost without his mobile phone. It had slipped out of his pocket when he was looking over a factory roof and had smashed to smithereens on the ground below.

"Hello," Nicole's mother said.

"Hi. It's Brad. Can I speak to Nicole?"

"Just a minute," she said.

A few minutes later, she came back to the phone. "I'm afraid Nicole doesn't want to speak to you."

Brad could not believe it. "Is this some kind of joke?"

"No," she said. "I'm sorry. Bye."

He put the phone down and stared at the graffiti on a wall. What the bleeding hell was going on? He had only phoned to arrange a time and a place to meet. Something must be wrong. Perhaps Nicole was ill.

He caught the bus to Nicole's house. If she was dumping him, he wanted to see her face-to-face. By the time he knocked on her front door, he was feeling angry. How could she have gone off him in such a short time? She had been mad about him the last time they met.

Nicole's father opened the door. "Hello, Brad.

"Hello, Andy," Brad said. "Can I see Nicole?"

Nicole's father spread his hands. "Nicole doesn't want to speak to you?"

"Why?" Brad asked. "It'll only take a minute."

"I can only tell you what Nicole said. I asked her to speak to you, but she won't."

Sod her, Brad thought. "Women. I'll never understand them."

"Me neither," Nicole's father said."

Brad said goodbye and caught the bus home. He was more confused than angry. If Nicole wanted to finish with him, she could have at least spoken to him. It was too confusing for words, but if that was the way Nicole wanted it, then that was how it was going to be. Sod her.

*

Nicole was sitting in her bedroom, looking out of the window. She felt very angry about what had happened to her and could not wait for the police to catch the animals and send them to prison. How anyone could do what they did to her, she had no idea. It was beyond her understanding. She had always imagined rape to be horrible, but she had not realised just how horrible. She had been hurt and humiliated and had feared for her life. Even now, in the safety of her bedroom, she still felt frightened that they would come after her again. She also felt degraded and mentally scarred.

Her mother walked into the bedroom with a cup of tea. "How are you feeling?"

"All mixed up."

Her mother placed the cup on the windowsill. "What do you mean?"

"The older I get, the less I understand about people and life." Nicole picked up her cup of tea. "Why does God allow such wickedness as rape and murder? If I were God, I would kill the bad people. Life would then be so much better."

"There are no answers to such questions," her mother said. "Even if the world was full of good people, there would still be pain, suffering, old age and death. And I know all about old age."

"You're not old, Mum."

"I feel it. How are your cuts and bruises? Do they still hurt?"

"Yes, but not as much." Her vagina and inside still hurt, and her breasts were still covered in green and yellow bruises. She had received several cuts and bruises when she fell through the roof. The cuts on her inner thigh and on her arm were deep and should have been stitched up, but she had not felt up to going into hospital.

"Drink your tea," her mother said. "You wasted the last one."

Nicole took a sip. "How long will it take to catch them?"

"I don't know," her mother said as she straightened the duvet and patted it as if it were alive. "The police are looking for them now. I wish you had spoken to Brad. It wasn't his fault."

"I know it wasn't. I just don't want to speak to anyone."

Her mother sat down on the bed and sighed. "Do you want to talk about what happened?"

"I've told you what happened. I was tied up for two days and raped repeatedly by five men."

"I know it's distressing, but the doctor said it would help to talk about exactly what happened."

"Well, I don't want to talk about the details." Nicole sipped her tea. Since the rape, she had been reliving every detail as if her life depended on it. From the second she opened her eyes in the morning to when she fell asleep at night, all she could think about was her ordeal.

"Angela, Linda and Sheryl have phoned," her mother said.

Nicole spun around, spilling her tea. "You didn't tell them, did you?"

"No. I promised I wouldn't say anything. I told them that you would phone them when you felt a little better. You mustn't be ashamed of what happened. It wasn't your fault."

"I know. Just don't tell anyone. I'll tell them in my own good time."

Her mother patted her arm. "Why don't you come down and watch the television? It's not good for you to sit in your room all the time."

"Don't fuss, Mum. I'm all right." She was far from all right. She was depressed and was full of anger and pain.

*

Brad could not get Nicole out of his mind. One minute, he had the girl of his dreams and was planning a holiday with her; the next minute, nothing: no girl and no holiday. It did not make sense. Why had she gone off him so quickly? He had to know why she had dumped him. It might be a misunderstanding that he could clear up. On his third day off, he took a bus to the university. Perhaps one of her friends could explain to him what had happened.

He did not want to be seen by Nicole and was relieved to see Angela walking on her own away from the university entrance. He walked towards her. "Hi, Angela."

"Hello, Brad," she said.

"Have you seen Nicole?" he asked.

"No. She hasn't been to any tutorials for a few days. I phoned, but she was too ill to speak to me."

Brad had not realised she might be ill. "What is she suffering from?"

"I don't know. Her mother didn't say."

"She didn't want to speak to me either," Brad said. "I don't think she's ill."

Angela frowned. "What do you mean?"

"I went to Nicole's home when her mother said that Nicole didn't want to speak to me. Her mother didn't say anything about Nicole being ill. Her father didn't either."

"Well, she is ill," Angela said. "The reason why she doesn't want to speak to you is probably because she's dumped you."

"Why would she dump me?" he asked. "And why didn't she say it to my face?"

"I don't know. And it's never easy to dump someone." Angela looked at her watch. "I'll have to go. She was probably too embarrassed to tell you to your face."

"I suppose so," he said.

Brad said goodbye and made his way home. He had never been so wrong about a woman before, and it unsettled him. He had been falling in love with Nicole. He lit a cigarette. No. He had already fallen in love with her. There was an ache in his heart that told him that he was still in love with her.

While having a drink in The Lighthouse public house that evening, he came to the conclusion that Nicole had been playing games with him. She had just been pretending to like him, and she might not have been a virgin. She probably makes a habit of pretending to be inexperienced and tells all her boyfriends that it was her first time. But even if Nicole had been acting, he still missed her. It was going to take him a long time to get over her.

Chapter Eight

It was eleven o'clock in the morning. Nicole was sitting in her front room opposite Detective Constable Ebans. He was about fifty and was tall and thin. He was asking her the same questions he had asked before.

"No," Nicole said. "I have not remembered anything else. I've told you everything."

DC Ebans closed his notebook and leaned back in his seat. "We've reached a dead end. We have no more leads to follow. The place you were kept in was burned down, and you can only tell us their first names, that they were West Indian and might drink at The Old Mill public house."

"Isn't that enough?" she asked.

"No." He opened his notebook. "John, George, Sam and Vic are very common names. Toss is probably a nickname. We know of criminals with these names who are West Indian, but we can't question them or arrest them without more evidence. You can't arrest a man just because his name's George. If only they had not used condoms when they raped you. We might then have been able to get a DNA match."

"I'm relieved that they did use condoms," she said.

"Oh, yes. I didn't mean ..." He spread his hands. "I do say some foolish things sometimes."

"Why do you think they used condoms?" she asked. "I would not have expected them to have bothered."

He puckered his lips and twisted them to one side. "It could be because they're married or have girlfriends and don't want to pass anything on to them. Or one or more of them had AIDS or a venereal disease, and the others didn't want to catch it. I don't really know. It could be just careful planning on their part. It's almost impossible to prove rape without a witness and a DNA profile, and because you had a shower and your mother washed your clothes, we have no DNA evidence. Your mother even washed your trainers." He stood up. "I'm sorry I haven't been able to catch them."

"So am I," she said.

The detective left, and she sat in the front room thinking. Her wounds had healed, and she had recovered physically but not mentally. Her mother had told her to pull herself together, but it was easier said than done. She was very depressed and had almost lost the will to live. All her feelings, except hate for the men who had raped her, had died. She now had no desire to do anything. Even eating was an unpleasant chore.

Her mother walked into the room. "I thought I heard the detective go. Are they any nearer to catching them?"

"No. I don't think they'll ever catch them." It was the first time she had acknowledged that the rapists would never be caught. She could not bear that. They had to be caught. She began to cry.

Her mother sat down beside her and put her arm around her shoulders. "It's about time you cried. You have only cried once."

"I ... cry ... every ... night," Nicole said between sobs.

"I've never heard you," her mother said. "It's good to cry."

"I'm getting even more depressed, Mum. I think I need the stronger tablets, even though they make me feel strange. And I want some sleeping tablets. I hate lying awake at night."

"I've got the stronger tablets in the kitchen." Her mother kissed her on the cheek. "And I've got the sleeping tablets. I think the tablets will help. You can't just sit here all day and every day. You have to start living again."

"I don't feel like doing anything."

"What about your studies? Angela said that she would help you catch up."

"I don't feel like studying, but I suppose I will have to do something. I'll see how I feel with the new tablets. If I feel up to it, I'll go on Monday."

"I'm sure it will help," her mother said. "Why don't you tell your friends what happened? They'll then understand why you feel so bad."

"I will eventually tell them, but I don't want you saying anything, Mum. Don't ever tell anyone what happened."

"I won't. Don't worry. Why don't you go out with your friends this weekend? It'll do you good."

"I'll see how I feel."

*

It was one o'clock in the afternoon. Brad was playing snooker with Carl. Brad leant over the snooker table and took aim with his cue. He needed to sink the black ball to win. "Watch this."

Carl leant on his cue. "I am."

Brad took the shot and gave the white ball a touch of bottom right. The black ball hit the side of the pocket and rolled into the centre of the table. "Fuck it. It wiped its feet and came back out again." He was annoyed. It would have been the first time he had beaten Carl two out of three.

Carl potted the black. "Easy-peasy. Fancy another two out of three?"

"Go on then," Brad said. "Your break."

Carl broke, and a red slipped into a pocket. The black was over a hole. "What skill?" Carl said.

It was not going to be Brad's night. "You're a lucky bastard."

"Are you still seeing Man?" Carl asked as he took aim at a red ball.

"On and off."

It had been over three months since Brad had seen Nicole, and he was almost over her, almost but not quite. Manjit, his latest girlfriend, helped to ease the pain. He called her Man. She had big tits and was sex mad. She was probably having sex with half a dozen other men, but he was not bothered. She was always there for him when he needed her. All he had to do was give her a call.

Dan walked up to their table. "I thought I'd find you in here, Brad."

"What do you want?" Brad asked.

Dan leant towards Brad and whispered, "Wayne's in some sort of trouble. I think he's been pushing drugs on someone else's turf."

"That's his bad luck," Brad said. "What does he expect me to do?"

"I don't know," Dan said. "Wayne just wants to talk to you. He's waiting at the back of the snooker hall."

Brad chewed his lip. It must be serious if Wayne was too scared to come into the snooker hall. He handed Dan his cue. "Play my hand until I get back." Brad walked towards the door. He felt annoyed. God knows what Wayne expected him to do. He walked out of the snooker hall and lit a cigarette. It was Wayne's fault for dealing in drugs.

"Hi, Brad," Victoria shouted as he walked down the side of the snooker hall.

"Hi, Victoria," he shouted. Victoria, a tall, slim blonde, had a crush on him. She would be all right if she had a different face. She was standing with a man. He was probably her new boyfriend. She changed boyfriends like he changed his socks.

There was no sign of Wayne at the back of the snooker hall. He looked about. "Come on. Where are you? Stop messing about."

There was no reply.

As he went to walk back down the side of the snooker hall, his foot kicked something. He looked down. It was a gun. He picked it up. It was probably an imitation, although it felt and looked real.

A Police car drove down the other side of the snooker hall and stopped. As two policemen climbed out, Brad threw the gun into a pile of rubbish and climbed the fence.

"Don't be a fool," one of the policemen shouted.

Brad was a good runner, and he soon lost them. He slowed down to a walk. Why were the police at the back of the snooker hall? Maybe they were looking for Wayne. And why did Wayne want to talk to him? He walked to Wayne's house and knocked on the door. Wayne's mother answered the door. "Is Wayne in?"

"No. He's taking the dog for a walk." She closed the door in his face. She was a miserable bugger.

He walked home, had a quick wash in the bathroom and changed his shirt. The run had made him sweat, and he was fussy about his hygiene. He would hate to smell of sweat. He walked out of the bathroom and leaned out of the landing window. The girl next door never closed her bathroom window, and he had often seen her naked. She had beautiful tits. Her bathroom window was open, but there was no sign of her.

A movement in the corner of his eye turned his head. Three policemen were climbing over his back fence. He ran downstairs, grabbed his coat and opened the side door. The side gate was locked, and there was no sign of anyone. He was hidden from the back garden by a shed, and so he was able to climb through a hole in the fence into the next door's garden without being seen. He walked around the back of his neighbour's house and climbed over their fence.

When he walked onto his road, about fifty metres from his house, he looked back. Three police cars were parked outside his house. He put on his cap, walked down an alleyway and took stock of the situation. Why were the police after him? Could it be something to do with Wayne? No. It was more likely because of the gun. They had probably seen him holding it. But how did they know who he was? They had been about thirty meters from him and so could not have recognised him. Victoria. She had seen him and must have told the police. His mates would never tell the police anything. Like him, they had no time for the police. Their policy was to deny everything.

He stopped at a corner and kicked a beer can. "Fuck it." His fingerprints would be on the gun. Someone could have used the gun in a robbery, and he would get the blame. It could have even been used to kill someone. He lit a cigarette and tried to decide what to do. He could not go home or to the snooker hall. He needed to speak to Wayne, but it was too hot around this area at the moment. He caught the bus to the centre of Birmingham. His mate John, who lives in Nechells, might be able to put him up for a few days.

Chapter Nine

Nicole, Sheryl, Angela and Linda walked out of Aston University. Nicole now wished she had not agreed to have a party at her home. The tablets she was taking made her feel drowsy, but seemed to be helping and enabled her to continue to study for her degree. She was functioning more like a robot than a human being.

"Let's forget all our troubles tonight," Sheryl said. "I, for one, intend to get pissed. What about you, Nicole?"

"I think I will as well." Nicole tried to smile. She hated being a killjoy. If only she could forget about the rape and get on with her life. It was only when she was drunk that she could forget, and that was only for a short time. She stopped walking. She was sure that the man walking towards them was Brad. He was wearing a blue cap. She had never seen Brad wearing a blue cap. It was him. She recognised his walk.

The bus came around the corner, and Brad broke into a run. He could just make it to the bus stop. He stopped. The woman staring at him looked just like Nicole. She looked different somehow. She had short hair, but it was her. Why was she staring at him as if he were a ghost? He was about to continue running for the bus, but hesitated. She looked sad. Sod it. It would not do any harm to say hello. He walked up to her. "Hello, Nicole. Long time no see."

"Hello, Brad." He looked as handsome as ever.

"Hello, Brad," Angela said. "I didn't recognise you in your cap."

He felt that he had to say something. Even though Nicole had lost eight, she still looked beautiful. "I saw a sold sign on your house. Did you move to get away from me?"

Nicole smiled. Talking to him had made her realise how much she had missed him. "No. I live in Sutton Coldfield now."

He could not tell whether she was still interested in him or not, but he needed to know. He had thought that he was over her, but seeing her today made him realise that she still meant a great deal to him. "Pity. I was going to offer to walk you home." It was a subtle hint, but she might pick up on it.

"It's about time you got a car," Linda said. "You could have given all of us a lift."

Nicole wanted to see Brad again, but he would want sex, and there was no way she could even let him touch her. Even a kiss would be out of the question.

"What are you doing tonight, Brad?" Sheryl asked.

"Nothing." He could not tell them he was on the run from the police.

"Then come with us," Sheryl said. "We're going to a party at Nicole's, and we're short of men."

"I don't know." He looked at Nicole. He could not tell whether she wanted him to go with them. It would be nice to talk to her again, and he might find out why she had dumped him. "I could do with going to a party, but ..."

"That's settled then," Sheryl said. She grabbed his arm. "The taxi's here. You can come with us."

Nicole was pleased that Brad was coming to the party. She would like to talk to him and find out what he was doing. She often thought about him. She should tell him what had happened to her, but she was not sure she could.

Brad was dragged into the taxi by three laughing women. He glanced at Nicole. She looked sad. She could be upset because he was going to the party. The only way he was going to find out was by talking to her. If he found out that she did not want him at the party or had a boyfriend, he would leave. He did not want to make things awkward for her.

Nicole sat in the front of the taxi, and Brad squashed in the back with the others. Nicole could not even bear a man to touch her, and she would not be able to sit close to one. In her mind, even though she knew that it was not true, she felt that all men were evil and capable of rape.

The taxi stopped outside a huge house in Sutton Coldfield. He frowned. It could not be Nicole's house. "Isn't this where you live, Angela?"

"No," Angela said. "Although I don't live far from here."

They all climbed out of the taxi.

As Nicole walked up to her front door, she began to feel anxious. All the bad feelings were returning and filling her mind. She opened the door. She needed a drink.

Sheryl grabbed Brad's arm and led him into the grandest house he had ever been in. It was even posher than Angela's house. The hall was bigger than his lounge at home. "How can you afford to live here, Nicole?" he said, but she was already running up the stairs.

"Don't worry about Nicole," Sheryl said. "She'll be all right when she's had a drink." She pushed him into the large, empty lounge. "Help yourself to a drink and let anyone in who calls. We're going to get changed upstairs."

There were no cans of lager or beer in the cocktail cabinet, so he poured himself a whisky and walked about. The house was fantastic, and the furniture was the best that money could buy. There were also several expensive-looking antiques dotted about. He walked into the large kitchen. Food was laid out on a large table. He then noticed a stack of about a hundred cans of lager. He finished off the whisky and picked up a can. The house must be worth over a million pounds. How could Nicole's parents afford this?

*

Nicole took a long drink of lager and sat on her bed. She felt drained of energy. She always felt tired from when she got up to when she went to bed.

The rapists had taken away the spring in her step. She now walked and moved like an old woman.

She had everything she could want except happiness. Her bedroom was large and fit for a princess and contained a fridge full of cans of lager. She had heard what Sheryl had said about her needing a drink. It was true. The tablets she was taking helped to stop her from turning suicidal, but it was the drink that enabled her to function. Without the drink, she would not be able to force a smile onto her lips, socialise or do her degree. Even with a drink, life was still an effort.

After two cans of lager, she felt more able to cope. She had been told not to mix alcoholic drinks with her tablets. She looked in the mirror. She looked worried, and her new hairstyle made her look old. Would she be able to talk to Brad? Yes. She had to. She needed to.

*

The doorbell rang. Brad was on his way to the front door when Linda, Sheryl and Angela came walking down the stairs. They were all dolled up. He left them to see to the guests and stood looking out of the window. He was not in the mood to socialise. He had too much on his mind, although he wanted to talk to Nicole. If she had a new boyfriend, he would like to know what he looked like. He was probably rich. He looked about. He also wanted to know how her parents could afford to live here.

*

Nicole took a deep breath, finished off her third can of lager, picked up another can and walked out of her bedroom. Some of the guests were sitting on the stairs, talking. She smiled at them as she walked downstairs. It was not going to be easy to talk to Brad. He might not understand. She saw him standing in the lounge, staring at the fish tank with a can of lager in his hand. He was a very handsome, sensitive man and would probably understand.

What little confidence she had suddenly disappeared, and she no longer felt up to talking or socialising. She walked into her father's study. If she told Brad about the rape, he would want to know the details, and she was not sure she could tell him. She had not told anyone the details. She switched on the CD player and sat in her father's swivel chair behind his desk.

She lived in a beautiful house and had everything she needed. She had new clothes and all the money she could spend. She would be happy, or at least be able to cope, if she were not so depressed. The tablets she was taking made her feel unreal. Life was bearable at the best of times and unbearable without the tablets. They said that she would eventually get better. She was not so sure. She felt that she would never be happy again.

Sheryl walked into the study and put her hands on her hips. "What are you doing in here? I've just walked all around the house looking for you."

"I don't feel like talking to anyone."

"What about Brad? He's standing on his own like a poor lost soul."

"I was going to talk to him, but I chickened out. I find it difficult to talk to men."

Sheryl walked over to her and hugged her. "You'll eventually get over it. It'll take time, but you will recover, and talking to someone like Brad will help. Shall I get him? You can talk in here."

"I don't know." The thought of talking to a man made her feel anxious.

"Go on," Sheryl said. "It'll do you good."

"Okay."

*

Brad had a drink. The lounge was now half full of guests. They were all in their twenties and were probably students. He had another drink and emptied the can. He was sitting in the kitchen next to the lager. At this rate, he would soon be drunk.

Sheryl walked up to him. "There you are." She took his arm. "Come on. Nicole wants to talk to you."

She led him out of the kitchen, across the lounge, along the hall and into a room that looked like a study. Nicole was sitting behind a large desk.

"I'll leave you to it," Sheryl said, and she stepped out of the room, closing the door behind her.

"What did you want to talk about?" he asked.

"I didn't. It was Sheryl's idea." She lit a cigarette. It was silly. Why could she not admit to wanting to talk to him?

He walked over to a fish tank. "Someone likes fish." He lit a cigarette, sat on a high-backed Elizabethan chair and looked at her. She was staring at the fish. She looked nervous. "Do you have a boyfriend?"

"No."

He was surprised. He took a drag on his cigarette. Something was not quite right. Perhaps she was upset about something he had done. Maybe someone had told her that he had been two-timing her. "Why did you dump me? Was it something I said or did? One minute, you thought I was God's gift. At least, that's the impression I got. The next ..." He spread his hands. "You dumped me."

"It wasn't anything you said or anything you did." She glanced at him and returned her gaze to the fish tank. Her father had bought three fish tanks, hoping they would help her relax. It was going to take more than watching fish to calm her nerves.

He twisted the cigarette between his fingers. This was all very strange. If he had not upset her, something else must have, but what? She was definitely upset about something. He decided to change the subject. "How long have you lived here?"

"About six weeks."

"Did your old man win the lottery?" he asked.

"Yes."

He almost dropped his drink. "How much?"

"Two million, I think."

"Bloody hell," he said. "It's no wonder you dropped me. I suppose you've got loads of rich boyfriends now."

"Don't talk like an idiot," she said. Even though she knew Brad was not a threat, she still felt anxious in his presence. "Could you get me a can of lager, please?"

"Yes." She seemed really upset by what he had said. She was nothing like the person she used to be. "I could do with getting drunk." He left the room, walked to the kitchen and picked up four cans of lager. On his way back to the study, he bumped into Sheryl, literally. "Hang on, Sheryl. Don't run off. Something's happened, hasn't it?"

"What do you mean?" she asked.

"To Nicole."

"Has Nicole said anything to you?" she asked.

He shook his head. "No. What's the problem?"

"I don't know," Sheryl said. She shrugged and walked off.

Something had happened. He was now sure of it. But what? And he was sure that Sheryl knew what it was. According to Nicole, it had nothing to do with him. It was a bit of a mystery. And why would Sheryl want him to talk to Nicole? He decided to let Nicole tell him in her own good time. What cheered him up a little was knowing that Nicole did not have a boyfriend.

He walked back into the study, placed three cans on the desk and opened one. "You've lost weight. It doesn't suit you." He hoped she did not have AIDS.

She opened one of the cans of lager and took a drink. According to her therapist, it would help her to talk to a man. Even though she felt like running upstairs, she decided to stay and talk. Maybe it would help. Her therapist was convinced that when she began to get better, it would happen quickly. Nicole did not believe it would. She felt that she was slowly going mad.

They sat in silence for a while.

He began to look through a stack of CDs. The one playing at the moment was a bit dated. He looked at the empty CD case. It was Barbra Streisand. "Who is Barbra Streisand?" he asked.

"They're my father's CDs," she said.

He began to look through them. "Good God. Des O'Connor. A Christmas Album. Bing Crosby. And who the bloody hell is Jane McDonald?"

"She's a good singer. It's a good CD." She had often listened to it.

He put it on, and Jane McDonald began to sing, One Moment in Time. He leaned back in his seat and listened. It was not too bad. At least she could sing. He felt he had to say something. "What is your father doing now? I bet he doesn't work at the Rover anymore."

"No. He's gone into business with his brother, my uncle. They sell security systems."

"Oh." He took a drink. "Can I stay the night?"

She stared at him. "I suppose so. Why do you want to stay the night?"

He decided to tell her. At least it would be something to talk about. "I'm on the run. The police are after me."

She was shocked. "What for? What have you done?"

"Nothing. I found a gun. I threw it away, but the police saw me holding it, and I had to leg it."

She suspected that he was telling her a yarn. "Why didn't you just tell them that you had found it?"

He took a long drink. There was nothing like free lager. "You know what the police are like. I was arrested once for something I didn't do. They'll fit anyone up given half a chance."

"I didn't know," she said. "You never told me."

"It was before I met you." He lit a cigarette. She seemed to be relaxing a little.

"What was it that you didn't do?" she asked.

"I was fifteen. A seventeen-year-old started a fight with me, but I won, and I cut his face. When his mother found out, she sent her boyfriend, an ape-like creature, to beat me up. This bloke was over twenty stone, and he grabbed me outside my house. My old man came out and had a go. This bloke threw my old man to the ground and broke his ribs. I hit the bloke and broke my fist. I then kicked him off my old man. My old man hit him with a large spanner, and between us, we saw him off. And even though there were a dozen witnesses, the police arrested the three of us. Me and my old man were charged with GBH. They eventually dropped the charges, and we were bound over to keep the peace. I don't trust the police an inch. They knew that we were innocent and that the thug was to blame, but they didn't care. All they wanted was to get a conviction."

She hated any form of fighting. "How's your studying going?"

"It isn't."

"Why?"

"Do you really want to know?"

"Yes."

"I was going out with a young woman at the time, who packed me in for no apparent reason, and it floored me. I haven't been able to concentrate since. I was pretty keen on her."

She looked down at her drink. "There was a reason."

Then tell me what the fuck it is, he felt like saying. Jane McDonald was singing, I'll Never Fall in Love This Way Again, which was very appropriate.

They sat in silence for a while.

It was obvious that she was not going to tell him the reason why she dumped him. "Do you still play the violin?"

"Yes." She stood up and walked to the door. "The bedrooms are all accounted for, but you can sleep in here if you want to. You'll have to be out early. My parents are coming back from holiday tomorrow."

"Thanks."

She opened the door and turned to look at him.

There were tears in her eyes, and she looked as if she was about to cry. He began to worry about her. "Have I upset you?"

"No."

"Then why are you so upset?"

She felt she had to tell him. "I did not dump you. There was a reason why I stopped seeing you."

He did not have a clue what the reason could be. "Are you going to tell me? I would like to know."

She took a deep breath. "I was raped." She stepped through the door, closed it behind her and ran upstairs. Perhaps he might now understand.

*

Nicole had gone before what she said had registered. He stood up. "Bloody hell." He wanted to follow her, but decided not to. It had obviously been difficult for her to tell him. He sat down and stared unseeing at the wall. So that was why she had dumped him. It was not because of the money or because she had met someone else. She had been raped. "The poor sod."

*

Nicole lay on her bed, crying for several minutes. The rape was once again vivid in her mind. She could remember every detail. All the pain, fear and humiliation came back. Why did men rape women? It was the vilest of crimes and was even worse than a physical assault. And why were the bastards still free and not in prison? Surely, if the police tried hard enough, they could find them. She had told them their names and the area where they lived.

*

Brad decided to get another drink and something to eat. He had not eaten since breakfast. He felt sad that Nicole had been raped, but was pleased that she had not dumped him because she had gone off him. There might be a chance that she still fancied him. He hoped so. The feelings he had for her were still very strong.

He walked into the lounge. The party was now in full swing. The music was loud, and some of the guests were dancing. He walked into the kitchen and filled a plate with food. He had the last three chicken legs, picked up a can of lager and sat on the worktop. He had a good view of the dancers. One woman was almost falling out of her dress.

One of the dancers smiled at him. She was dark-haired, small and had a little girl's figure. She looked Chinese. He winked at her. She beckoned him to dance with her. He shook his head and pointed to his plate of food.

She walked towards him. "Are you on your own?"

"Yes."

"Thank God for that. I seem to be the only woman without a bloke." She picked up a bottle of lager and sat next to him on the worktop. "I expected there to be loads of single men. This is the first party I've ever been to that's made up entirely of couples." She smiled at him. "Almost. Do you have a girlfriend?"

"Not as such." He did not count Man as a girlfriend. "Why haven't you got a boyfriend? You've got a cute little figure."

She squeezed his knee and smiled. "Thanks. My steady has gone back to London. He's packed in his studies. Are you a student?"

"No."

She frowned. "Why haven't you got a girlfriend? You're too good-looking to be unattached."

He smiled. "I'm in between engagements."

"If you've just had a row with someone at the party, tell me," she said. "I know most of the women, and they'll go mad if I pinch one of their blokes."

"I didn't come with anyone," he said. "I was just at a loose end, and a party seemed like a good idea."

"Good." She held his arm as if to lay claim to him.

Sheryl stopped in front of them. "I see you've got yourself a bloke, Tina."

"Yes," Tina said. "He's lovely. We've only just met, and we haven't got around to names yet. Sex first, then names."

Brad smiled. It looked as if it was going to be an eventful night. He could do with sex. He had not had a bit for three days.

"His name's Brad," Sheryl said as she walked off.

"Hello, Brad," Tina said.

"Hello, Tina," he said.

"Do you fancy me?" she asked.

"Yes."

"Good. You can come back to my flat. It's only small, but it's cosy."

"What would you have done if you hadn't met me?" he asked.

"Gone to bed alone. It was very inconsiderate of Bill to walk out on me like that. Everything was perfect. I'll be honest with you. I need sex at least twice a week; otherwise, I'll go mad. I also need a boyfriend, but sex comes first. To me, sex is almost as important as food. Does it shock you?"

"No. I also regard sex as important, and I go mad if I can't get any. I also need a place to sleep. I'm homeless at the moment."

"That's settled then," she said. "You can stop at my place for as long as you like. Do you want to dance?"

"No. I'm not one for dancing." He still had two chicken legs to eat.

"Then wait here." She slipped off the worktop. "I love dancing. I'll be back in a bit."

He sat eating, drinking and watching her dance. She was a very sexy woman. Despite the offer of sex and a place to live, he was still worried about the police and why they were after him. He was also worried about Nicole. Being raped had obviously knocked her about. If he found out who had raped her, bones would be broken.

*

Nicole was sitting on her bedroom windowsill, smoking. The window was open, and the bedroom light was off. She had spent many nights watching foxes, badgers and cats wandering around her large back garden. There was no sign of them at the moment, and she sat watching the bats darting back and forth. Her house was near farmland and in an ideal place to watch wildlife of all sorts.

She took a drag on her cigarette. She was smoking and drinking too much. It had been nice talking to Brad. Although not at first. She had been all on edge. But later, after they had talked for a while, she had relaxed a little. When she had told him that she had been raped, he had looked shocked, and there had been a worried look in his eyes as if he cared for her. She then realised that she had not told him not to tell anyone about the rape. She would have to go down when most of the partygoers had gone and tell him that she did not want anyone to know about what had happened to her.

It might be a good idea to see him again. It might help if she talked to a man. If she were going to recover, she would have to talk to men. The only man she felt relaxed with was her father.

Someone knocked on the door. "Yes." She was hoping it was Brad.

The door opened, and Sheryl walked in. "I wasn't sure if you were asleep. How are you feeling?"

"The same. I'm surprised that I managed to talk to Brad. I've told him that he can sleep in the study."

"Are you thinking of getting back with him?" Sheryl asked.

"No. Definitely not. I want him as a friend. I'm not ready for a boyfriend. I just feel that it will help me to talk to a man."

"It will," Sheryl said. "I'd better tell you. Tina has latched onto him, and you know what that means. She's sex-mad. She'll even have sex with a woman if she can't get a man."

"That's all right," Nicole said. "If he's sexually satisfied, he might not come on to me."

"Are you going to see him again?" Sheryl asked.

"Yes. I think so."

"Then you had better tell him," Sheryl said. "He'll no doubt be leaving with Tina."

Nicole had not realised. "Tell me when he's ready to leave, and I'll come down."

"Okay. I'd better get back."

Sheryl left the room, and Nicole looked out of the window. There was something she was going to give Brad. She could not remember what it was. She drew on her cigarette and stubbed the nub in the ashtray. What was it? It was a present of some sort. A book. That was it. It was a book.

*

A fat woman walked over to Tina, who was sitting next to Brad on the worktop. "Do you want a lift, Tina?" she asked.

"Yes. Is there room for Brad here?"

"Just about," the fat woman said. "We'll be leaving in a few minutes."

While Brad was waiting in the hall for Tina to say her goodbyes, Nicole walked down the stairs. "Thanks for inviting me to your party," he said. He would like to see her again, but he did not want to push his luck. It would not do his ego any good to be rejected for a second time.

"Are you leaving now?" she asked.

"Yes. I've got a lift." He was hoping that she did not know he was going to sleep at Tin's flat.

"Here." Nicole handed him a bag. "It's a book about dinosaurs. I bought it for you just before we broke up."

We did not break up, he felt like saying. You dumped me. He took the bag. "Thanks." She was already walking upstairs. "I'll see you around," he shouted.

She turned around on the top of the stairs, smiled and nodded. "Yes. Bye." She walked into the safety of her bedroom.

It was the saddest smile Brad had ever seen, and his heart went out to her. She must still be suffering.

"Did Nicole tell you?" Sheryl whispered into his ear.

He nodded. "I'd like to help, but I don't know what to do."

She took a business card off a table. "This is Nicole's phone number. Give her a call, and if she's awkward, don't be put off. She needs to talk to a man. Oh, I nearly forgot. Don't tell anybody. Apart from Nicole's parents, only you, me, Linda, and Angela know."

"Don't worry. I won't say a thing." He was pleased that Nicole had told him. Perhaps she did think something of him.

Tina grabbed his arm. "Come on, lover boy. Bye, Sheryl."

"Bye," Sheryl said.

Brad joined about ten people in the back of a large van. There was very little room, and he was crammed between two drunken blokes. He was worried that one of them would be sick, and knowing his luck, it would come in his direction. The fat woman was a maniac driver and threw the van around the corners as if she were trying to commit suicide. He was glad when they arrived at Tina's flat, and he was able to get out.

Tina took his arm and led him into an old Victorian house that had been converted into flats. "She drives like a madwoman, doesn't she?" she said.

"Yes," he said. "Is this where you live?"

"Yes. It's not much, but it's home."

He followed her upstairs and into a small room that contained a single bed, a wardrobe and a dressing table.

"This isn't a flat; it's a cupboard," he said.

"It's all I can afford." She closed the door and took off her coat. "I share a lounge, a bathroom and a kitchen with six other students." She threw herself into his arms and kissed him on the lips. Her tongue was everywhere.

He began to feel her breasts. They were bigger than he had thought. A nice handful. He squeezed her erect nipples.

She pulled away and took off her sweater. "My tits aren't big, but I've been told that they're nice."

He began to get undressed. "They're just right." She was now down to her pants. "You have a perfect figure."

"Do you come quick?" she asked.

"No. I try to make it last at least a minute."

She took a condom out of the dressing table drawer and handed it to him. "I come quick, especially when I fancy a bloke, and I fancy you. But I usually come two or three times, so don't stop on my account. You can fuck me for as long as you like. I love to be fucked."

He rolled the condom onto his erect penis, and she pulled him down onto the bed on top of her. She opened her legs and guided his penis into her. She was very small, and her head was pressed against his chest. He gripped her shoulders and thrust into her.

"Bloody hell," she screamed. "Oh. Bloody hell. Oohhhh."

"You almost deafened me," he said when she had stopped screaming.

"I always scream when I come," she said. "Everyone in the building knows when I'm being fucked."

He had drunk a bit too much, but he eventually climaxed as she screamed for the third time. His body shuddered with pleasure as her screams rang in his ears. A few seconds later, he flopped down on top of her tiny body. It was like having sex with a ten-year-old.

"You're too heavy," she said, and she pushed him off her.

For a short time, they lay side-by-side, staring at each other. She had dark, smiling eyes. "You're a right character," he said.

"I know." She kissed him on the lips and turned around. "Put your arms around me. I like to sleep like this."

With her little body curled up in his arms, he began to fall asleep. It had been one hell of a day.

*

It was three-thirty, and Nicole was still awake. She decided she would have to take a sleeping tablet. She hated taking tablets, but she also hated thinking, and it was always worse at night. She took the tablet and crawled into bed. They were very strong and usually worked within about fifteen minutes. It was nice speaking to Brad. Sheryl said that she had given him her number. If he did not call her, she would call him. She then remembered that he was not living at home and was on the run from the police, and she did not have his mobile number. If he did not phone her, she would ask Sheryl to contact Tina and get his mobile number. He was bound to call her.

Chapter Ten

Brad woke up at ten-thirty. Tina was asleep. She woke up as he was getting dressed.

"Are you going out?" she asked sleepily.

"Yes."

"When will I see you again?" she asked.

"Tonight. I might be late."

"Come any time you want." She smiled with her eyes closed. "As long as it's inside me."

He left her flat in Winson Green, put on his cap, which he hoped would serve as a disguise, and walked to Ladywood. He needed to speak to Wayne to find out if he knew anything about the gun and why the police were after him. It was unlikely to be Wayne's gun, but if it was, why had he left it lying at the back of the snooker hall? And what trouble was Wayne in? Maybe he needed a gun to protect himself. Dealing with drugs was a very dangerous line of work.

Five hundred metres from his house, he met up with Dan and Carl.

"Where the bloody hell have you been?" Dan asked him.

"I've been lying low. The police are after me."

"I'll say they are," Carl said. "They're all over the place. What the fuck have you done?"

"Nothing." Brad began to worry. It must be serious if the police were going to so much trouble to find him.

"Come on," Carl said. He smiled and pushed Brad on the arm. "You must have done something."

"I haven't done a bloody thing."

Dan offered Brad a cigarette. "If you haven't done anything, why are the cops after you?"

Brad took the cigarette and lit up. "I don't know. I was thinking about giving myself up, but I'm now having second thoughts. I'd first like to know what I'm supposed to have done. Could you find out?"

Dan spread his hands. "What the fuck can we do? The cops won't tell us anything. There was trouble at the snooker hall, and we thought you had something to do with it."

"What trouble?" Brad asked.

"We don't know," Carl said. "There were cops everywhere, so we went to The Lighthouse for a drink. We guessed it to be a fight."

"Try and find out what's going on," Brad said. "Ask around. I'll meet you at The George tonight. Be there about nine. Someone's bound to know something. And tell Wayne that I want a word with him."

"We'll see what we can do," Dan said. "Is it worth a drink?"

"Yes. I'll see you at nine."

Brad left them, walked to the bank on the High Street and took fifty pounds out of his account. He was reluctant to spend his savings, but he had to live. He was a bundle of nerves and was constantly looking about for officers of the law. Just possessing a gun was now a serious offence. His gut feeling was that there was more to the situation than possessing an illegal firearm and that somehow Wayne was involved.

He was starving, so he headed for the café he used. As far as he knew, no one knew that he used this particular café. There were dozens of people about, and he was able to lose himself in the crowds.

*

It was ten o'clock in the morning. Nicole was sitting in the lounge of her house with her therapist, Miss Hastings. Nicole lit a cigarette and looked out of the window. Miss Hastings was beginning to get on her nerves. She seemed to say the same things every time they met.

"I think we've covered everything," Miss Hastings said. "Are you listening to the relaxation tapes?"

"Yes." Nicole was lying. She hated the tapes. All they did was send her to sleep.

"Good," Miss Hastings said. "You'll find that in time, they will help. Are you getting a good night's sleep?" Miss Hastings was about sixty, very small and had a false arm.

"If I take sleeping tablets."

"Are you managing to cope with your studies?" Miss Hastings asked.

"Just about. I go to all the lessons at the university that I should go to, and I'm up to date with my work." She was copying most of Angela's work.

"It would help if you talked to men." Miss Hastings looked at her watch. "I think I'll have to go."

"I talked to an old boyfriend yesterday," Nicole said.

Miss Hastings looked surprised. "I am pleased. Are you going to see him again?"

Nicole shrugged. "I think so."

"It's a good start." Miss Hastings stood up. "You'll only begin to recover when you talk about exactly what happened. I know it's painful and embarrassing, but it will help, and you know that you can always talk to me."

Nicole showed Miss Hastings out and went for a swim. It was only a forty-five-by-twenty-foot pool, but it was inside the house and warm. She swam slowly up and down. Would it really help her recovery to talk about what had happened? She doubted that it would, but it was worth a try. Anything was worth a try. All she was doing at the moment was existing, and she would rather die than live the rest of her life like this. Who could she talk to? Not to her parents, or to Angela or Linda. She might be able to tell Sheryl or Miss Hastings. Maybe she could tell Brad. Maybe.

*

After Brad had eaten his breakfast, he looked through the book that Nicole had given him. It was full of colour pictures of dinosaurs and had a price tag of twenty-five pounds. He put the bag under his coat and zipped it up. He would have to give Nicole a call and thank her for the book. If she had not been raped, they would still be together. If he knew who the bastard was who had raped her, he would make sure that he never raped another woman. He chewed his lip. When Nicole recovers, they might be able to get back together, although it could take months or even years to get over being raped.

He walked out of the cafe and walked up to a public phone box. He hated using public phone boxes, but he had left his mobile phone at home. He looked about. There was no sign of the law. Before he phoned Nicole, he phoned his place of work. The police might have already been there.

"Hello," Peter said.

"It's Brad. I thought I'd give you a call."

"I was wondering where you had got to," Peter said. "The police are after you. What have you been up to?"

"Nothing. Did the police say why they wanted to see me?"

"No. They asked me to phone them when you arrive for work, but don't worry, they won't be hearing from me. I've got no time for the cops."

"I won't be in for a while," Brad said. "Could you keep my job open for me? I want to find out what it's all about before I go to the police."

"Sure, Brad. Don't worry about a thing."

Brad hung up the phone and felt in his pocket for the business card with Nicole's number on. It would be just like him to have lost it. Two black men were waiting outside the phone box. They looked like thugs. One was very tall and slim; the other was tall and muscular.

The muscular thug opened the door. "Are you Brad, a friend of Wayne's?" he asked.

"Yes," Brad said. "What do you want?" As he spoke, he realised that he should not have told them who he was. He should have claimed to be someone else. If they were undercover cops, they had him trapped in the phone box.

The muscular thug pulled a handgun out of his coat and pointed it at Brad's chest. "They were friends of mine," he whispered.

"No," Brad shouted.

The thug shot him twice in the chest. The force of the bullets slammed him against the phone box, and he slumped to the ground. The two thugs walked calmly away. He had been shot in the chest. He would soon be dead. He probably had only seconds to live. If he were going to be saved, he would have to phone for an ambulance.

A woman appeared and looked down at him. "I saw what happened," she said. "They shot you."

"Could you phone for an ambulance?" he asked.

"Yes, but you'll have to move. I can't reach the phone."

He was lying half in and half out of the phone box. He sat up and looked down. There were two holes in the front of his leather coat, but he could not see any blood.

"If you just move to one side," she said. "I'll be able to reach the phone."

There was something wrong. He should be in severe pain and covered in blood. He breathed deeply. His chest hurt, but he had no problem breathing. He stood up. He did not feel as if he was dying, and where was the blood?

A crowd was gathering outside the phone box. "Are you all right, mate?" a man asked.

Brad opened his coat, took out the book that Nicole had given him and examined his chest for the two bullet holes. He was probably bleeding internally. He opened his shirt and examined his chest. There was not a mark on him. Not even a small hole.

The woman looked at his chest. "They must have missed. You are a lucky man."

"Did someone shoot at you?" a man asked. "I heard the sound of gunshots."

Brad pushed his way through the crowd and ran down the road. The police would soon be here. He ran down several side roads and stepped into a public house. There was no way that the thug had missed. He had aimed the gun at his chest from a distance of about two feet. The black thug had obviously used blanks, but why? Why would they want to shoot him with blanks? It did not make sense. Unless they just wanted to frighten him. If they had, they had done a very good job of it. He had been terrified.

He bought a drink and sat down outside the pub. There was no sign of the police or the black men. It took him thirty minutes and two drinks to calm down sufficiently to think clearly. Being shot was a terrifying experience. He frowned. If they had used blanks, he would not have felt the bullets hit him, but he had felt the bullets hit his chest. The force of the bullets had knocked him against the phone box. It felt as if he had been kicked, and his chest still hurt.

A thought occurred to him as he took out his cigarettes, and his eyes and mouth opened wide. No. It was not possible. He put the cigarettes back into his pocket, opened his coat and took out the book. It was possible, and if it had happened, it would explain why he had felt the power of the bullets but was unmarked. He took the book out of the bag. Good God. It had happened. It was unbelievable. The book had saved his life. There were two holes in the front of the book. He opened the book. Three-quarters of the way through, he found two bullets wedged into the pages. He closed the book and stared, unseeing, at his half-finished drink.

"Fucking hell," he said. "Fucking hell. Fucking hell." The book had saved his life. If he had not been carrying the book, or if it had not been a thick book, he ... "Fucking hell." If Nicole had not given him the book ... "Fucking hell."

He sat for about an hour, drinking and thinking. Something heavy was going down. The two black men had meant to kill him, but why? He had not done anything to anyone that warranted being killed. He lit a cigarette, his fifth since sitting down. The only thing he could come up with was that it had something to do with Wayne. He could vaguely remember the black man with the gun mentioning Wayne's name.

Could they be friends of Wayne and think that he was after Wayne? Or did they think that he was a friend of Wayne's? Something must have happened to Wayne, but what? And why would the two men want to kill him? It must have something to do with the gun he found. His main worry was that when the black men found out that he was not dead, they would come looking for him. From now on, he would have to keep a lookout for the police and black thugs.

At six o'clock, he left the pub and caught the bus to The George public house. Perhaps Dan and Carl had found out what was going on. He then remembered that he had intended to give Nicole a call. When he got off the bus, he walked across the road to the public phone box. Phone boxes now made him feel nervous. As he pushed in Nicole's number, he kept looking about. If he saw even one black man, he intended to watch his every move.

"Hello," Nicole said.

"Guess who," he said.

"Oh, it's you."

"You recognised my voice then."

"Of course."

She did not sound too happy to hear from him. "I only phoned to thank you for the book. It saved my life."

"How can a book save your life?"

"It's a long story, and I don't want to bore you." He could tell that she did not want to speak to him, and he was getting fed up with being treated as if he had raped her. "Are you nasty to everyone, or is it just me?"

"I've told you that it has nothing to do with you. Being raped has made me ill."

"I don't know what to say or do," he said. "I know you've either had a breakdown or you're having one, and I'd like to help, but I don't intend to let you treat me like shit. I don't deserve it."

"I'm sorry," she said.

Her apology sounded hollow, but it was probably all he was going to get. "I'll see you around."

"Wait. I don't mean to be nasty. I'm just not feeling very well at the moment. I am sorry. You just don't understand."

"I know. I would like to try to understand. Is there any way that I can help? I don't mind talking, listening or taking you out for a walk in a park. Or anything."

"Do you really want to help?"

"Yes."

"My therapist thinks I should talk to a man. I just don't want you to read anything into it."

"I'm not a complete idiot. I won't come on to you. I just want to help."

"Maybe you can help," she said. "Could we talk?"

"Yes. When would you like me to call?"

"Anytime tomorrow. Make it after nine when my parents are out."

"I'll see you about ten." He said goodbye and stared at the phone. She was in a very bad way. Being raped had all but destroyed her. She was now a shadow of her former self. All her zest and vitality had gone. She was …

Someone knocked on the phone box's door, and he jumped six inches into the air. It was a group of young girls.

"Come on," one of them said. We haven't got all day."

He took a deep breath. He would have to be more careful. Anyone could have crept up on him. He opened the door. "Keep your knickers on, love."

She pushed past him. "I don't wear any."

"A likely story," he said, as he looked about to make sure that the police or black men were not moving in on him.

"Show him," one of the other girls said.

The girl in the kiosk lifted her dress and showed her bare backside. He blew out his cheeks. "Bloody hell. I could do with a slice of that."

She pulled down her dress and smiled. "In your dreams."

He left the girls, who looked to be about fifteen, giggling and walked to The George public house. It was early, but he did not have anywhere else to go. He sat at a table outside the public house, drinking and thinking over what had happened. It was unreal. His life had been meaningless and boring until he met Nicole. It had then gone berserk. He fell in love; his girl was raped; he found a gun; the police think he had committed a crime and want to arrest him, and two black men have tried to kill him.

It was nine-thirty when Dan and Carl turned up.

"Where the bloody hell have you been?" Brad asked.

"Just get the drinks in," Dan said. "I need one bad."

When they were seated at a table outside the public house with their drinks, Carl said, "We were followed."

Brad frowned. "You were followed. Why would someone follow you?"

Dan spread his hands. "We don't know."

Brad began to worry, and he looked up and down the road. "Did you lose them?"

"Yes," Dan said. "They were real pros. Carl spotted them first. It's a bloody good job he did."

"Are you sure you lost them?" Brad asked. He was now very worried.

"Yes. Don't worry." Dan emptied his glass. "I hope we're going to get another drink for what we've been through. We're a little short of cash."

Brad took a twenty-pound note out of his pocket. "Tell me what happened. How did you know that you were being followed?"

"I'll get the drinks," Dan said. "I've never needed a drink so much." He picked up the twenty-pound note and walked into the pub.

Carl finished off his drink and offered Brad a cigarette. "We were followed by two blokes. They were wearing jeans and leather coats. The two blokes who asked us about you were black, but the blokes who followed us were white."

Brad lit his cigarette. "I don't know why they would be following you." He suddenly realised what Carl had said. "Who asked about me?"

"We don't know who they were. We've never seen them before. They spoke to us outside the snooker hall."

"Was one of them tall and slim, and the other tall and stocky?" Brad asked.

Carl nodded. "They asked us if we'd seen you. We said that we hadn't. They said that if we find out where you are and tell them, there would be a hundred quid in it for us."

Brad could not believe it. "Why would the two blacks be after me? I haven't done anything to them."

Dan sat down with the drinks. "They think that you killed two of their mates. Their bodies were found at the back of the snooker hall on the night you went there to speak to Wayne. It's been on the news. Everyone's talking about it. From what we can gather, the police also think that you killed them."

Brad felt confused. "I didn't kill anybody. Why would they think I killed them?" He then remembered the gun. "Fuck it. They think I killed them because I found a gun at the back of the snooker hall. I must have left my prints on it."

Dan frowned. "You found a gun. What did you do with it?"

"I threw it away. Someone must have used that gun to kill the two blokes."

"You could be right," Carl said. "Someone must have killed them just before you went to see Wayne."

Brad took a long drink. "This is fucking ridiculous. I've got the two blacks and the cops after me, and I haven't done a fucking thing. I think them white blokes who followed you were cops, undercover cops."

"You could be right," Carl said. "We saw them by accident. I was looking out of the back of the bus in case the two blacks were following us. I saw the two white blokes in a car. I noticed them because I'd seen them in the snooker hall. When we got off the bus, they followed us. To lose them, we had to run through the market."

Brad sat thinking. "They were definitely cops. I think Wayne has something to do with this. Have you seen him?"

They both shook their heads.

"I think he's somewhere around Norway," Dan said. "His mother said that he got a job on a cruise liner."

"Why would he suddenly go off on a cruise?" Brad asked. "It would help if I knew what he wanted to speak to me about. And what about his drug dealing?"

"He's given that up," Dan said. "I think them black blokes were also after him. They asked if we'd seen him."

Brad was beginning to put two and two together. "I think Wayne killed the two men. Were the blokes who died black?"

"Yes," Carl said.

"How the fuck could Wayne kill two men?" Dan asked. "Wayne didn't carry a gun."

"I know how Wayne got the drop on them," Brad said. "Wayne told me that he had trained his dog to go for anyone who pulls a knife or a gun on him. Wayne must have got the gun from the two men and shot them, and because I picked up the gun and left my prints on it, the police think I killed them. Fucking hell. I've got the cops and a drug gang after me. Do you know who this drug gang is?"

Dan shook his head. "No. We'll try and find out."

"What are you going to do, Brad?" Carl asked.

"Keep out of sight. Do either of you have a mobile phone?"

"No," Carl said. "I lost mine when I was pissed, and Dan dropped his in the canal."

"Typical," Brad said. "If I have to contact you, I'll phone the snooker hall."

They stood up and walked onto the road.

Brad looked up and down the road. There was no sign of the police or the blacks. "I'll phone the snooker hall in a couple of days."

"Okay," Dan said. "Watch your back."

"I will."

Brad walked down the road. Dan and Carl walked in the opposite direction. After walking for a few hundred metres, Brad stepped behind a hedge and looked back to see if he was being followed. He could not afford to be careless from now on. His life depended on it. There was no one following him, and he walked to the bus stop.

It was eleven-thirty in the evening when he knocked on Tina's door.

"Who's there?" Tina asked. She sounded half asleep.

"It's me, Brad."

She opened the door. "You're late. I was asleep."

He walked into the room and closed the door. "I'm sorry, but I didn't have a key." As he began to get undressed, she climbed into bed. She was wearing pants and a bra. "If I'd have known how good you would look, I'd have been here hours ago."

She looked at him from over the duvet. "You can take that look off your face. I'm poorly, so it's no sex for five days."

He climbed into bed and put his arms around her. "Sod it. I was hoping to make you scream."

"I'm going to see my parents tomorrow, so I'll be away for a few days," she said. "There's a key on the dresser, so you can come and go as you please. Just be ready to fuck me like mad when I get back."

"I can't wait," he said.

*

To please her parents, Nicole had watched a video with them. It was an exciting science fiction film, and it had taken her mind off things for a while. She was now sitting on the windowsill in her bedroom, looking out of the open window and smoking. The badgers were in the garden. They were quite large and headed straight for the food that she had put out for them. The foxes did not get a look in when the badgers were out. The badgers were vicious and fought over the food. She could understand how they were related to dogs.

Brad said that he would call tomorrow. She looked at the luminous dial on her watch. Today. It was nearly one o'clock. She took a drag on her cigarette and blew the smoke out of the window. She was determined to tell Brad everything, even the horrible details.

She frowned. How could a book save Brad's life?

Chapter Eleven

It was just before eleven o'clock in the morning when Brad walked up Nicole's drive. It was an hour's bus ride from the centre of Birmingham and a fifteen-minute walk from the bus stop. He looked about. The detached house was as big as a hotel and was set in several acres of land. They had certainly moved up in the world. Nicole opened the door before he was able to ring the bell.

"You made it then," she said.

"I think so." He walked into the hall. "I'll feel better when I've had a cup of tea."

She closed the door. "Who said you were going to get a cup of tea?"

He reached for the doorknob. "I'm off then. I can't survive without a cuppa."

She smiled. "Come on. I suppose you can have a cup of tea." She walked towards the kitchen. "I'll show you where everything is. You can make it yourself."

He followed her across the spacious lounge to the kitchen. "It must be great living in a house like this."

She pointed to the tea and coffee. "There's lager, beer and wine in the fridge and stronger stuff in the cocktail cabinet. You'll have to help yourself. I hate getting drinks for people."

He took a can of lager out of the fridge and sat down at the kitchen table. "How are you feeling?"

"Don't ask."

He stared at her. She looked drawn and tired. "Are you getting better, getting worse or staying the same?"

"I'm getting worse." She sat down and spun a teaspoon around on the table. "I think I'll end up going mad."

He took a drink of lager. "These things take time. Will talking about it help?"

"My therapist thinks so."

"Then let's talk about it."

"I don't want to." She leaned back in her chair and looked at him. He had not had a shave and looked untidy.

He took another drink. "Do you want to talk about anything?"

"No."

"I'd be no good as a counsellor," he said. "I feel like kicking you up the arse."

She smiled.

"Was that a smile?" he asked.

She shrugged. "Maybe. You used to make me smile a lot. You were always a daft sod."

"Why don't you have a drink?" he said. "It might help you to relax."

She opened the fridge and took out a can of lager. "I'm drinking too much."

They sat drinking in silence for a while.

He felt frustrated. She was obviously unhappy, and talking might help, but he could not think of anything to talk about. "What are we supposed to be doing?"

"Talking."

"Are we supposed to be talking about the rape?" he asked.

She nodded.

He looked at her. "What happened? Where were you when you were raped?"

"I was waiting for a bus to go to college."

He frowned. "It happened on the main road in daylight?"

"No. I was tied up and taken in a car to a derelict house."

"Bleeding hell. What happened?"

"I was raped."

"I know that. I meant, how did he rape you?"

"I don't want to talk about what happened."

"Why?"

"I just don't feel able to."

"Have you told anybody the details about what happened?"

She shook her head. "I've just told the police that I was raped. I don't see what difference knowing the details will make."

He did not know either. "Hundreds of women must get raped." He took a drink. "This is no good. We should be doing something."

"Such as?"

He spread his hands. "I don't know. Anything."

She sighed. "I don't want to do anything. I've been taken to Disneyland, Paris, the Grand Canyon and New York. It was a waste of time. I did not enjoy myself."

"Well, we can't just sit here," he said. "Do you have a swimming pool?"

She nodded.

"I thought so. Let's go for a swim. We can strip off and jump naked into your pool. You don't have to worry. I won't rape yo ... Oh, bloody hell. I didn't mean to say that. I ... Oh, fuck it." He took a long drink. "I just wanted you to know that you can trust me."

"Don't worry," she said. "I don't think I'll ever trust anybody again. Not completely. You can have a swim if you like."

"No." He took a drink. "I only wanted to have a look at your bum."

She did not smile. Sometimes, smiling was impossible. The way she was getting progressively worse was getting her down. It would be better if she were dead.

He stood up. "We can't sit here all day. You can show me the garden."

"Okay." She placed her can of lager on the worktop and opened the back door. She used to enjoy so many things. Being raped had killed her enjoyment of life. Or was it the tablets? She had a choice. She could take the tablets and live without feelings or suffer the full force of the pain, worry and anxiety. No. She did not have a choice. She would not be able to live without the tablets and had to continue taking them.

He followed her into a huge garden. "Bloody hell. This is a park, not a garden. I hope you're not going to ask me to mow the lawn."

At a snail's pace, they walked around the garden. They walked past three greenhouses, through a small wood containing about fifteen large trees, past a pond, and back to the kitchen. He helped himself to another can of lager and sat on a swinging seat on the patio.

She picked up her half-empty can of lager and sat on a non-swinging seat next to him. It was always quiet in the garden. All she could hear was birds singing and a distant lawnmower. He seemed to be worried about something. She had a feeling that it was not about her. Perhaps he had problems. He was chewing his cheek and deep in thought.

He noticed her staring at him and smiled. "It's nice here." He offered her a cigarette. "Why can't you talk about how you were raped?"

She took a cigarette. "What's the point?"

"Fucked if I know." He offered her a light from his lighter and lit up. He watched her. Could she keep a secret? He reckoned she could, even though she was ill. "If I told you something, could you keep it to yourself?"

"Yes."

"I don't want you to tell anyone, and I mean anyone," he said.

"I won't. What secret?"

"I'm wanted by the police and by a gang of drug pushers."

"You told me that the police were after you," she said.

"Did I? Oh, yes. I forgot."

She stared at him. "Why are drug pushers after you? What have you done? You're not pushing drugs, are you?"

"No. I don't have anything to do with drugs." He stood up, walked into the kitchen and returned carrying the bag that contained the book of dinosaurs that she had given him. He handed her the bag. "Have a look in that bag."

It was the bag that she had put his present in. She opened it. It contained the book she had given him. "I don't understand. This is the book I gave to you."

"Take it out and open it," he said.

She took the book out. There were two holes in the front cover. She opened it and found what looked like two bullets stuck into the pages. "Are these bullets?"

"Yes."

She looked up at him. "I don't understand. Why did someone shoot two bullets into the book?"

"I was carrying it at the time." He took a drag on his cigarette. "I had it shoved inside my coat."

She stared at him for a few seconds. "Someone shot you?"

"Yes. Two black men tried to kill me. If I hadn't had that book inside my coat, I'd be dead. I put it under my coat because I hate carrying plastic bags. Look." He pushed his fingers through the two bullet holes in his coat.

She stood up and then sat back down. The strength had left her body. She was shocked. "Why did they shoot you? Why do they want to kill you?"

"I think it's because they think I killed two of their gang. The police also think I killed them."

"Why?"

"Because my fingerprints are on the murder weapon."

"What murder weapon?"

"A gun. I picked up the gun after the two men had been shot."

"You must be worried sick," she said.

"I'm shitting myself if you want to know. As soon as the drug pushers find out that I'm not dead, they'll come looking for me."

She looked out across the garden. The book she had given him had saved his life. If she had not given him the book, he would be dead. It was a chilling thought. Life was very strange. She could see him putting the book into his coat and the men shooting him, and all because he had picked up a gun belonging to someone else.

She took a drag on her cigarette. If she had not sheltered in the doorway from the rain, she would not have been kidnapped. She had passed her test and was about to buy a small car, which she intended to share with her mother. If she had not failed her test the first time, she would have already bought the car and would not have been in the doorway on that particular day. The rapists would then have kidnapped someone else. She would not have been raped and would now be enjoying life. She would be having sex with Brad, playing her violin, and ... But what about the other woman who would have taken her place? She shivered. They would have raped her and probably killed her. If she were a man, she would go after them. They deserved to die.

Brad's stomach was doing somersaults and making groaning sounds. "Could I scrounge a sandwich?" he asked.

"Yes." She stood up. "Are you hungry?"

"I'm almost starving to death."

"I'll cook you something." She walked into the kitchen and put a TV dinner into the microwave.

He followed her and sat down at the table.

She filled up the kettle. "I'll make us a cup of tea. We can't keep drinking lager." She switched on the kettle and looked at him. He looked worried. "Where are you going to live, and what are you going to do about money?"

"I've got somewhere to sleep." He decided not to tell her that it was with Tina. "And I've got some money, although it's not much."

The microwave pinged, and the kettle boiled. She placed the meal in front of him and made them a cup of tea. "If you are ever short of cash, I'll be pleased to help."

"Thanks." He began to eat the meal. The food was heavenly

She sat down and watched him eat. "I think I would be able to cope if it weren't for the nightmares."

"What nightmares?"

"I was thinking out loud. It's not a nightmare as such. It's a very strange dream."

"What do you dream about?" He was too hungry to stop eating and had to talk with his mouth full of food. She certainly knew how to pick her times to have a meaningful discussion.

"About being stalked by someone. I don't see them, but I know they're there. I wake up screaming."

"Fucking hell." He took another mouthful of food and watched her sipping her tea. He had had a couple of nightmares. They were very frightening. "How often do you have the nightmares?"

"Every time I go to sleep, although I don't always end up screaming."

"Fucking hell." He did not really know what to say. "It must be a ..." He nearly said a nightmare and corrected himself just in time. "... pain."

"It is. I hate going to sleep." She suddenly realised that he had finished his meal. "You shouldn't eat so fast. Do you want anything else?"

"No." He did, but he did not want to appear greedy.

"There's ice cream, tinned fruit and cheesecake," she said.

He licked his lips. "Mmmmmm. Go on, then."

She stood up. "What do you want? Ice cream, fruit or cheesecake?"

"All three. I haven't eaten properly for a few days."

She placed the food on three plates in front of him and sat down. She had told him about her nightmares almost without realising it. He was the first person she had told, other than her parents. It was silly not to talk. "If I could see who was stalking me in my dreams, it wouldn't be so bad."

He swallowed a mouthful of ice cream. It was cold on his sensitive tooth, and a pain shot through his jaw. "Perhaps it's the bloke who raped you." He put another spoonful of ice cream into his mouth on the opposite side to his sensitive tooth.

"Blokes." She broke off a small piece of cheesecake and popped it into her mouth. She should eat more proper meals.

He stared at her and swallowed the ice cream. "Blokes. How many?"

"Five."

"Five. Fucking hell." He would have to find more appropriate adjectives to use.

"They grabbed me from behind and bundled me into the boot of a car. I didn't see their faces."

He ate the food while she talked.

"They tied me up and blindfolded me. I've been tested for VD and that, and yesterday I had a letter saying that I don't have AIDS."

He picked up the dish of peaches. "Did they get a DNA match?"

"No. They used condoms. They used me like a blow-up doll. When I escaped, they destroyed the evidence. They even burnt down the building where I was kept."

"No wonder you have nightmares." He started on the cheesecake.

"One of them almost ripped my breasts off my chest and forced me to suck him off and swallow it, and all the time, I knew they intended to kill me when they had finished with me."

He pushed the empty cheesecake dish away from him and picked up his cup of tea. She had been through hell, and he really felt for her. "The bastards. The world is full of trash like them. They need a taste of their own medicine."

"I was all right at first," she said. "It was the nightmares that did it. I'm now on tablets. To get to sleep, I have to take a sleeping tablet. I'm taking tablets for my anxiety and for depression. I get panic attacks if I have to travel on my own, or if I think about sex or if a man gets too near to me. I'm supposed to be improving, but I'm not. Without the tablets, I couldn't live."

"Did the police catch them?" he asked.

"No. I feel cheap and soiled."

"You shouldn't feel like that," he said. "You are not cheap or soiled."

She sipped her tea. "Thanks for being kind."

He leant back in his chair. It was no wonder she had a breakdown. "I'm not being kind. Being raped does not change the woman one bit. She is still … you know. The same person she was. She has done nothing wrong. If I were marrying a woman and she told me that she'd been raped, it wouldn't make any difference. Being raped does not make a woman unclean."

She was able to relax with him a little better now that he knew what had happened to her. "It doesn't stop how I feel."

"No. It'll take time. These things always do."

"We both have our share of problems," she said. "What are you going to do about your problems?"

"Try and find a mate of mine, Wayne. He was the one who, I think, killed the two black men. If I can find him, I might be able to prove my innocence."

They talked about a few things over a can of lager, and after agreeing to see her tomorrow, he left and caught the bus back into the centre of Birmingham. He had things to do. He would not like to live this far from the centre of Birmingham, at least not without a car.

*

Nicole went for a swim. The feel of the water on her skin helped her relax. She had told him about the rape, but it had not made any difference. Maybe it would in time. She swam slowly up and down. He was a nice person, and she was glad that he would be coming tomorrow. She needed someone to talk to other than her girlfriends and parents. She was worried about him being chased by the police and drug pushers. It was the drug pushers she was more worried about. The police would arrest him, but the drug pushers would shoot him. She would hate for him to get shot.

*

Brad phoned the snooker hall when he got to the centre of Birmingham. None of his mates were there. It would be too dangerous to go anywhere near his house or the snooker hall, so he caught the bus to Tina's. She was sitting in the kitchen with two of her fellow students: a small, fat, red-faced woman and a tall, thin, long-haired man. He sat down with them and was given a cup of tea. Tina looked to be in a murderous mood.

"What's the problem?" he asked.

"My dad only gave me twenty pounds, and my tutors refused to accept my work," Tina said. "He called it rubbish."

"It's not that bad," the fat woman said. She had bright red hair and thick-rimmed glasses. "It's just a bit short."

After listening to them moaning about life, the lack of money and the large amounts of studying they had to do, they all went to The Sack of Potatoes public house for a drink. Tina was beginning to drive him mad, and he could now understand why her last boyfriend had left her. He would not be able to take much more of her weird moods. He left them drinking and moaning and phoned the snooker hall from the public phone in the hallway of the pub. "Is Dan there?" he asked the manager of the snooker hall.

"Yes. I'll get him."

"Hi, Brad," Dan said a short time later.

"Have you heard anything, Dan?" Brad asked.

"Yes. You won't believe it. If I were you, I'd emigrate. It turns out that the brother of one of the black men who were killed is the leader of a drug gang in Handsworth. They're willing to pay a thousand pounds to anyone who knows where you are."

Brad could not believe it. "The bastards. Have you heard anything about Wayne?"

"No. He's probably still in Norway."

"Couldn't you explain to this gang that I didn't kill anyone?" Brad asked.

"No way. Do you think I'm mad? If they thought that I knew anything, they'd kill me. I intend to tell them that I don't know anything. You'll need to be very careful. They're ruthless bastards. They paid a visit to your house."

Brad began to worry. "What happened? Did they do anything?"

"They roughed up your old man and Tim a bit, but nothing serious, so don't worry."

"The bastards." Brad was now very angry. "Where does this gang hang out?"

"I've been told that the leader's a bloke named George, and they usually hang around a pub named The Old Mill. I wouldn't go after them if I were you."

"What makes you think I would?"

"I know you, and normally I would help, but not against this gang. They claim to have a hundred gang members, and they have guns. I've been told that they've killed a couple of blokes."

Brad thought about how they had nearly killed him. "I can believe that. I'll have to go. I'm running out of change. Try to find out where Wayne is."

"I will," Dan promised.

Brad was angry, worried, frustrated and depressed. He wanted to kick the shit out of George and the two blacks who were after him. They had no right to hurt his family, but how could he go after a vicious gang armed with guns? He should have kept the gun he had found.

He walked back into the lounge and sat down. Tina was still in a bad mood and was now moaning about the weather. She was probably upset because she was having her period. He got drunk and fell asleep with his arms around Tina's little body. He felt frustrated in more ways than one.

Chapter Twelve

Nicole felt bitterly disappointed. She had told Brad the details about the rape, but she was still just as ill. It had not made the slightest difference. She was sitting in the lounge in an armchair, facing Miss Hastings, and drinking a cup of tea. She felt like telling her to piss off. She was still having the nightmares and still needed the tablets and booze to cope. If anything, she felt even more depressed. Her one hope of getting better had gone.

"It would help if you would answer my questions," Miss Hastings said. "I need to know how you're progressing."

"I'm pissed off if you want to know." Nicole stood up and walked over to the fish tank. "You said that if I talked about the rape, I would begin to get better. I told a friend all about the rape, and I'm still just as bad."

"I'm pleased that you're talking about what happened to you," Miss Hastings said. "But these things take time. It'll take weeks, even months, before you feel a difference."

Nicole turned and stared at her. "Months. I can't wait months. I want to get better now."

"It doesn't work like that," Miss Hastings said. "Each person is different, and each mental illness is different. Some people become ill over a period of months, and some, like you, due to a traumatic experience. The mind mends in a similar way to a broken bone, and all breaks, mental and physical, take time to heal. A mental illness is different to a physical illness in that whatever is causing the mental illness must be removed before a person can recover. If a man has a nervous breakdown because of the pressure of work, he must be relieved of that pressure first before he can begin to recover."

"What's making me ill?" Nicole asked.

"I wish I knew. The mind works in complicated ways. If a person becomes ill due to worry about their job, simply thinking about giving up the job can alleviate the worry. They will begin to get better if they get another job. I was hoping that talking about the rape was the key to your recovery. It could be. We'll have to wait and see. We can't rush these things."

"I hate being ill," Nicole said. "If I reduce my tablets, I go to pieces. I then keep dwelling on the rape and how near I came to death. My mind goes round and round and round."

"I wouldn't even think of reducing the tablets yet," Miss Hastings said. "You need to use the tablets as a crutch for a while. Then, when you feel that you are improving, you can slowly reduce them."

"I'm not improving," Nicole said. "I'm getting worse."

"You've made the first steps to getting better," Miss Hastings said.

Nicole frowned. "What steps?"

"You're talking to a man, and you've talked about the details of the rape. Do you still feel anxious when you're alone?"

"Not in the house, but I do if I go out. I take a taxi to college. My father bought me a car, but I can only drive it if someone comes with me."

Miss Hastings stood up. "I'm pleased that you're talking about your ordeal. When I see you again, I'm sure we'll see an improvement."

Miss Hastings left the house, and Nicole walked into the back garden. Even when she was alone, she felt safe in her house. It was her refuge. She felt a little anxious in the garden but forced herself to leave the house. She lit a cigarette and sat on a bench. Her parents, who worked in an office in Knowle, had never been happier. Life was so unpredictable. When Nicole had been happy, her parents had been depressed. It would be nice for them all to be happy. If she had a choice, she would give up her big house and all that she owned to be happy. Happiness was everything.

*

Brad left Tina's flat and, after phoning Nicole to explain why he would be late, he walked to his house. Having a sex-mad girlfriend was not all roses. He enjoyed sex at night but not in the morning as well. He was a once-a-day man. If Tina were going out early, she would wake him up for sex. To keep her happy, he fucked her whenever she wanted, but only climaxed at night. In the mornings and afternoons, he fucked her and played with her clitoris until she had screamed three times. The nights were different. He thoroughly enjoyed making her scream at night. He always slept better after sex. Nicole was the person he would really like to have sex with.

He lit a cigarette and put on his new yellow cap. He was getting near his house and did not want to be recognised. From what Carl and Dan had told him, his parents were worried that the thugs would return. He had made up his mind to go after the drug gang and cause them some grief. His family had always relied on him to protect them, and he was not going to let them down.

For twenty minutes, he hid in the front garden of one of the houses on his road and observed the comings and goings around his house. Everything seemed normal. He then saw Tim walk down the road and go into their house. It would be so much easier if they had mobile phones. They would then be able to keep in touch. Brad climbed over three fences and a wall into the front garden of the house next to his house. If the police appeared, he would have to make a run for it.

There was no sign of the police and so he climbed through the hole in the fence and let himself into his house through the side door. Tim was making a cup of tea. "Are you all right, Tim?"

"Fucking hell," Tim said. "Don't creep up on me like that. You scared me to death."

"Where's Mum and Dad?" Brad asked.

"They're living with Uncle John. Are you all right?"

"Yes. Why aren't they living here?"

Tim sat down. "You scared the shit out of me then. I thought it was them three black bastards again. They frightened us when they were here. I thought they were going to kill us. One of them had a gun. Mum and Dad are too frightened to live here anymore. And I'm living on my nerves."

"I want you to get a mobile phone so that I can keep in touch," Brad said.

"I'm going to live with Mum and Dad," Tim said. "You can phone us there. Dad is thinking of renting this place out until things calm down. I think Dad will sell it eventually. The three men who came here were the meanest bastards I've ever met. One of them was named George. Are you going after them?"

"Yes."

Tim shook his head. "Dad said that you would. You're a brave bastard. If I were you, I'd forget about them. You'll know what I mean when you see them."

"I've already met two of them. They tried to kill me." He pushed his fingers through the hole in his coat. "I was lucky."

Tim looked shocked. "Fucking hell. They shot at you?"

"Yes."

"They're obviously out for revenge," Tim said. "What I want to know is why you shot them two men?"

"I didn't shoot anyone." Brad looked out of the back door to make sure that the law was not moving in on him. "I've been set up."

"Then tell the cops," Tim said. "If this bloke George and his gang find out that you didn't kill them two blokes, they'll leave us alone."

"It's not as easy as that," Brad said. "I'll have to be going. Was Mum and Dad hurt?"

"They broke two of Dad's fingers and punched Mum in the stomach. Be careful. They'll do more than that to you if they get the chance."

"I intend to get in first," Brad said. "Have you seen my mobile?"

"Yes. It was in your room. Dad's using it."

"I'll have to get another one," Brad said. "When I get a mobile, I'll phone Dad and give him my number, and get yourself a mobile phone."

"I will," Tim said.

Brad said goodbye, left the house, and crawled back through the hole in the fence into the garden next door. He looked up and down the road. There was no sign of the blacks or the police. He ran down the road, had a quick look behind to make sure that he was not being followed and walked through the gully.

He began to seethe with anger. The bastards had terrorised his family, and for that, they were going to suffer. And because his family had moved away, he had no worries about reprisals, but first, he had to find out more about this drug gang.

He bought himself a mobile phone and called Dan at the snooker hall. "What have you found out?" he asked Dan.

"Not a lot. To be honest, we're too frightened to ask. One of their gang, a white man, is now supplying the drugs around here. From what we can gather, this gang is branching out. What are you going to do? You can't stay on the run for the rest of your life."

"I've got no choice if I want to stay alive. Have you seen Wayne?"

"No. He's vanished off the face of the earth."

"I'll phone you in a few days," Brad said.

Brad caught the bus to Sutton Coldfield and sat on the top deck thinking. Before he did anything about the gang of thugs, he would have to think things through. He could not afford to make any mistakes. He would have to find out where they lived, what cars they drove and how many were in the gang. It would be impossible to get the whole gang, but he could get the three bastards who had frightened his family.

*

Nicole was pleased that Brad came to see her every day, and she now felt relaxed in his company. She looked forward to seeing him and was glad that she had told him about the rape and the nightmares. She had expected the nightmares to end, but they were still as bad as ever. Talking about the rape had not made the slightest difference to her life. She would have to see what happened over the next few weeks.

She lit a cigarette and sat on her bedroom windowsill. She had been doing a great deal of thinking over the last few days. Brad, who was supposed to be visiting his family this morning, had vowed to get the men who had hurt his parents. She had offered to help. It might do her good to think about something other than the rape. She intended to have a word with her father to see if she could get a few gadgets to help Brad in his search for the men.

She had also considered searching for the men who had raped her. With Brad's help, she might be able to do it. If she could find out who they were, she could have them arrested. She might feel safer if they were in prison.

It was twelve-thirty. She walked out of her bedroom and into her parents' bedroom so that she could look for Brad. The security monitor was on. It was positioned above the bedroom door. By switching from camera to camera, she could see the lounge, the hall, the kitchen, the back garden and the drive. She switched the monitor off when she saw Brad walking through the gate. She ran down the stairs and opened the front door. "You're early. I didn't expect you until after one."

The gravel crunched under his feet. Nicole was making an effort to be friendly, but the pain in her eyes gave the game away. It would be fantastic to see her smile like she used to. She had a fantastic smile. "I didn't want you moaning at me for being late."

"I suppose you want breakfast?" she asked.

"Yes." He walked into the house, closed the door and followed her into the kitchen. "I'll cook it if you like."

"No. I don't mind. It gives me something to do. I've got it ready." She broke an egg into the frying pan. "You can make the tea."

He filled up the kettle and switched it on. "You look different. Is that a new hairstyle?"

"No. I've just tied it back off my face. I've only been to the hairdresser's once since I was raped. Did you see your family?"

"Yes. I saw Tim. My parents have moved. The bastards frightened them."

"Who did?" she asked.

"The black drug dealers."

"What did they do?"

"They threatened them, broke my dad's fingers, and punched my mother in the stomach."

"No wonder they were frightened," she said. "What are you going to do? Are you still going after them?"

"Yes." He put two cups on the table. "But first, I want to find out as much about them as I can."

She cooked his breakfast and sat watching him eat it. Yesterday evening, when Sheryl was going over the project they were doing, she told her about Brad and Tina.

"What's Tina like to sleep with?" she asked.

He looked up, expecting her to be angry. She did not look angry. "A scream, actually."

She smiled. "Wait until I tell Sheryl what you said."

He put the last piece of sausage into his mouth and leaned back in his seat. "I'm only sleeping with Tina. She's not my girl. If I didn't, I'd be out on the street."

"You don't have to explain to me." She made him another cup of tea. She felt that it was time to change the subject. "Have you met up with Wayne yet?"

"No. I don't think I'll ever see him again."

They walked into the back garden and sat on the patio, smoking and listening to CDs. They could sit without speaking. She had always been easy to get on with. "Did you ask your father about me working for him?" He was not too keen on going back to be a security guard.

"Yes. He's getting you an application form and some literature on what they sell. He wants you to train as a salesman. It'll mean travelling all over Great Britain. It could even mean travelling abroad."

"I don't mind." He took out his cigarettes. "I like the idea of being a rep. Will I get a car?"

"Yes, eventually, so you'll have to learn how to drive."

"I've already passed my test. Can you drive?"

"Yes." She took the cigarette that was offered to her. "I seem to remember telling you that I had passed my test."

"Did you?" He could not remember. "Do you have a car?"

"Yes."

"That's handy," he said.

"Why?"

"I want to go looking for the drug gang, and I don't fancy going on foot. You could drive me around. Are you up to driving?"

"Yes. I think so." She did not want to drive, but she would force herself. It would not be so bad with Brad in the car with her. "When do you want to go?"

"Today, if you like." He suddenly realised that he had lit his cigarette but not hers. He offered her a light. "Sorry."

She leaned forward, and he lit her cigarette. She inhaled and leaned back in her chair. "It's too late to go today." She did not really feel up to it. "I'll need to make sure that I'm insured and that the car is taxed. We could go tomorrow."

"Okay. I'll be here about ten. I've got a mobile phone. We'll be able to keep in touch now."

She stared at him. "Don't you get bored sitting with me?"

"Sometimes."

"Why do you come here every day?" she asked. "I look forward to you coming. I would just like to know why."

He took a drag on his cigarette. "I'm hoping that I can help you get better." He was also hoping to eventually rekindle their relationship. "I'd give anything for you to be back to the way you were."

She looked across the garden. "So would I. It would be wonderful to be normal again."

"Don't give up," he said. "You'll get there eventually."

She turned to look at him. "Do you think so?"

"I know so."

Chapter Thirteen

Brad was sitting in the kitchen of Nicole's house, and she was cooking him breakfast. It was twenty past ten in the morning. "How are you feeling?" he asked. She looked as she always did, sad and depressed.

"The same. I didn't get to sleep until four o'clock, and then I had my usual nightmare." She placed his breakfast in front of him, sat down and watched him eat. She had never known anyone to eat so much. It was a wonder he was not overweight.

"You need a haircut," she said when he had finished eating.

"It's part of my disguise." He took out his cigarettes. "Do you feel up to driving?"

"Yes. Where will we be going?"

"Handsworth." He offered her a cigarette. She refused. "The gang operate all over, but their home base is in Handsworth."

She frowned. "That's a coincidence. The men who raped me took me to Handsworth. I was going to ask if you would help me look for them. We could kill two birds with one stone."

"I don't see why not." He chewed his lip and then took a drag on his cigarette. "I thought you said you were blindfolded?"

"I was."

"Did you see their faces?" he asked.

"No."

"Then how can you look for them?"

"I know their names, and I heard them speak."

"It's going to be very difficult, but I suppose we can try." There was no way they would be able to listen to all the men in Handsworth, but he did not want to discourage her. "I haven't got much to go on either. All I know is that the drug gang's leader is named George, although I do know what two of them look like. We can drive around and see if we can see them. They might then lead us to the others."

"Did you say that the gang leader was named George?" she asked.

"Yes. Why?"

"One of the men who raped me was named George. It could be the same man."

"I doubt it. There are loads of Georges about."

"He's also black," she said. "He sounded West Indian, and he was the leader of the gang."

He sat thinking. "It is a bit of a coincidence. It's a pity you didn't see his face."

It was too much of a coincidence as far as she was concerned. She was convinced that the George Brad was after was the George who had raped her. "I heard him speak, and I'll recognise his voice. He had a very deep voice." She began to feel excited. If Brad identified the gang, all she had to do was listen to them speak.

Most West Indian men sounded the same to him, but he did not want to upset her. She was obviously keen to find the men who had raped her. He stood up. "Shall we make a move?"

"Yes." She stood up and picked up the car keys. "The car is insured. When we find these men, what are you going to do? Are you going to beat them up?"

He followed her to the garage. "Being over six feet tall and strong doesn't count for much today, especially when you're up against guns, knives and vicious thugs. The first thing I want to do is find out where they live. I then intend to follow them and look for the opportunity to do something. As yet, I haven't decided what."

"Sheryl borrowed my mother's car, so we'll have to use my car," she said. "My mother goes to work with my father. She works in my father's office in Knowle."

"Knowle," he said. "That's on the other side of Birmingham. Why don't you move and live over there?"

"We are. My father's looking for a house." She opened the garage door and unlocked the car. She could not wait to start looking for the men who had raped her, and when she found them, God help them. If she had her way, they would be sent to prison for life.

He stared at the car. He could not believe it. It was a Porsche. "My God. What a car." He had dreamed of owning a Porsche. "Are you a good driver? This is a very powerful car."

"I'm a very good driver." She was not going to tell him that she was feeling very nervous.

They climbed into the car, and she drove out of the garage and down the drive. She was driving slowly until she got used to it. She would much rather drive her mother's BMW.

"What about the house?" he asked. "Aren't you going to lock it up?"

"It locks automatically when we leave, and if the sensors do not locate anybody in the house, it sets the alarm."

"Very clever," he said. "I bet it's expensive?"

"It is. Most of what my father sells is expensive."

They drove around Handsworth for over two hours without seeing the two men who had attacked him. He was feeling aggravated and frustrated. Handsworth was a large place and was full of black people. It was going to be more difficult than he had expected. "Pull over her," he said.

She parked the car in The Garden Gate public house car park, and they sat down on a bench in front of the public house. She was not so nervous now and was enjoying the driving. "What are we going to do?"

"I don't know. Do you want a drink?"

"No, thanks. I'm probably already over the limit from what I drank last night." She could sense his despondency. "It could take years to find the men at this rate."

"I know. Driving around like this is a bit of a waste of time. At least we know the area now." He took out his cigarettes. "I think we'll need to look for these men at night. We'll probably find them in one of the pubs."

"We can go tonight," she said.

They sat smoking in the sunshine. Several people were admiring the Porsche.

It could be dangerous to visit the pubs in Handsworth, and he was reluctant to take Nicole with him. Parts of Handsworth were no-go areas for whites, but refusing to take her could spark off their first argument. "Handsworth is a dangerous place. I think I should go on my own."

"I want to go with you," she said. "In the pubs, I'll be able to listen to the men speaking. I need to find these men. We could ..." She was interrupted by Brad grabbing her hand. She pulled her hand away. She could not bear to be touched by a man. He was looking behind her. She turned around. "What's the matter?"

"We've got to leave."

A black car had pulled into the car park and had parked behind the Porsche. She watched two black men climb out, look at her car and then walk into the public house. "Are those the men who tried to kill you?" she asked.

"Yes." He stood up. "Let's go before they come out."

She followed him. "Why? It's taken us all day to find them."

"Just do it," he said. "We haven't found them. They've found us. We are now in serious trouble."

They ran to their car and climbed in. As she started the car, the two black men came back out of the public house. One of them pointed at her car. "They've seen us," she said.

"How fast can you drive?" he asked.

The two black men ran towards their car.

"Watch." She had forgotten how powerful the Porsche was, and the tyres squealed as she drove out of the car park.

"Be careful," he said. He clicked on his seat belt and looked behind. The black car containing the two black men was following them.

She drove over a bridge and turned right. "Are they definitely the men who shot at you?"

"Yes, and they're bound to be armed, so try to lose them."

"I'll do my best," she said. "It's not easy with all the tablets I'm taking."

Oh, no, he thought. He gripped the dashboard. He could probably drive better than her, but there was no way they would be able to change seats.

She drove up a hill and turned left at an island. "I don't know my way around here. You'll have to direct me."

He knew the roads. "Turn right."

She glanced in the rear-view mirror. The black car was now right behind them, and she was driving as fast as she could. Cars were parked all along the narrow road, making driving very difficult.

"Turn right at the bottom of the road," he said. "Not here." It was too late. She was already turning. "This is a cul-de-sac."

She braked as she turned and spun the car. The back of the car spun a hundred and ninety degrees, hit a lamp post, and they ended up facing the way they had come. The black car skidded to a halt alongside them.

One of the black men lifted a handgun, and Brad ducked down. "Drive off. Drive off."

The tyres squealed as she drove out of the cul-de-sac and down the road. The black car began to follow them. "I don't think I can lose them," she said.

He sat up and looked behind. "That was fucking close. Are you all right?"

"I think so."

They were approaching a 'T' junction.

"Right and right again," he said. "I don't want to worry you, but if they catch us, I think they intend to kill us."

She began to feel frightened. "Shall I drive to a police station?"

"No. Let me think." They were now driving at over sixty miles an hour. She was a good driver, but not good enough. "Straight over the island and straight on." They were heading back to Hamstead. If only he had a gun. He looked behind. They were right behind them. The two men were smiling.

They were approaching the main road.

"Which way?" she asked.

"Right." The traffic lights were on green. She took the corner at speed. She was doing very well, but there was no way they would be able to lose the black men. "Straight on. Take the right fork and go straight up the hill." They were now heading up Old Walsall Road. They had no choice but to drive to a police station. It would mean that he would be arrested, but it had to be done. He could not risk Nicole getting hurt.

She was doing eighty miles an hour, but the other car gained on them and then pulled alongside them. They were approaching the lights at the top of the hill. "What shall I do?" She had never driven this fast before.

The black man in the passenger seat lowered the window and poked a gun out. Brad ducked down. "They have a gun. We'll have to go to the police station. Turn right at the top."

She glanced to her right, saw the gun aimed at her, panicked and hit the brakes. The car skidded and swung toward the curb. She overcorrected, and the front of the Porsche hit the back of the black car. She fought to control the Porsche.

He braced himself. This was it. They were about to crash, and if they were not killed in the crash, the bastards would shoot them. The Porsche was jumping from side to side. As she began to regain control of the Porsche, the black car that was now in front of them overturned. "Watch it," he shouted.

She swerved and managed to avoid hitting the spinning car. She began to slow down. This time, she was easy on the brakes. They pulled into the curb and watched the rolling car in front of them demolish a traffic light and come to rest upside down.

"Fucking hell," he said. "Did you see ..." The black car burst into flames. "Fucking hell."

They sat watching the burning car. Several people stopped their cars and climbed out, but no one went near the burning car.

She could not believe what had happened. She had believed they were going to crash. "Did they get out?"

"No. I saw their bodies in the car before it burst into flames. Let's get out of here fast."

She turned right and drove along Walsall Road. "They must be dead."

"They are." She was driving too fast. "Slow down a bit. We don't want to be stopped by the police."

She was only in second gear and was doing over fifty miles per hour. She slowed down to forty. "The men who tried to kill you are dead. Are you glad?"

"Yes. It was them or us. They were trying to kill us." He began to relax. "They must have seen us driving around and recognised me."

"The Porsche is a bit conspicuous," she said. "We need a different car, and you need a disguise when we go back. I'll ask the girls at the university who are into acting to lend us some of their props."

He was amazed and stared at her. He had expected her to be frightened to death. "We don't have to go back." He was satisfied that the men who had tried to kill him were dead, and he would be happy to stay away from Handsworth for the rest of his life.

"We do." He seemed reluctant to continue the search. "We have to. We need to find George." She had to convince him to continue looking. She was determined to find the men who had raped her. "They might find out that you were involved and go after your family. One of the men could have contacted the gang on a mobile phone."

He sat thinking. "You could be right. My family have moved, but I'll give them a call and tell them to be careful." He lit a cigarette. "So, you want to go back to try and find George?"

"Yes. And I need your help."

"Aren't you frightened?" he asked. "We nearly died a few minutes ago. If they hadn't crashed, we would have been shot."

She examined her feelings. "I'm a little nervous, but I'm more frightened of not finding the men who raped me than being killed." What really terrified her was the possibility of never getting better. She would rather die than be ill forever.

She had helped him, and so he felt obligated to help her. "Okay, but this time, I'll wear a disguise, and we'll need to get a less conspicuous car. And I think it'll be better if I drive."

They parked the Porsche in Nicole's garage and climbed out. The car was badly damaged. The offside rear was smashed in, and the nearside front was damaged.

"Bleeding hell," he said. "What are your parents going to say?"

She shrugged and walked into the house. "I don't care. It was worth it."

He followed her into the kitchen. "What do you mean?"

"The car's insured. Do you want a drink? I need one."

"Yes." He leaned against the worktop. "I wasn't asking about the car. You said it was worth it? What did you mean? Did you enjoy what happened?"

"Yes." She took two cans of lager out of the fridge and handed one to him. "I was frightened, but I enjoyed it. When we were being chased, it was the first time I had felt normal and alive since I was raped." She opened her can and took a long drink. "I think I need to take revenge for what happened to me. If I don't do something, they will get away scot-free."

"The two blacks were probably not the ones who raped you."

"I know, but they were equally as bad. They were drug-dealing murderers, and they were trying to kill us. If we had not killed them, they would either have killed us today or continued looking for us. They could have taken down my car registration and eventually found out where I live."

She was right. He took a long drink. They would have to be extra careful from now on. "What we need is bulletproof vests and guns."

"My father sells bulletproof vests."

He was surprised. "Could he get us a couple of vests?"

"I'll ask him. You'll be seeing him tomorrow night to talk about the job."

"He'll want to know why we want bulletproof vests," he said.

"I'll think of some excuse. Do you want something to eat?"

"Yes. I love your cooking."

She smiled. "They are TV dinners."

He ate his meal and left her to have her daily swim. Before leaving her house, he had made her promise not to let anyone into the house she did not know. He was worried that the drug gang would trace the Porsche. While he was on his way to Birmingham centre on the bus, he phoned the snooker hall. Dan answered the phone. "I saw the two blacks who shot at me," Brad said.

"What happened?" Dan asked.

"They're dead."

"Fucking hell," Dan said. "How the fuck did they die? Did you kill them?"

"They were chasing us, and their car overturned and burst into flames. It'll teach them to mess with my family."

"Fucking hell," Dan said. "I've just been watching pictures of the burnt-out car on the television. I never dreamed that you would have had anything to do with it."

"The crash was unreal," Brad said. "I'll tell you what happened when I see you. Just keep it to yourself. Have you seen Wayne?"

"No, but I spoke to his girlfriend. She told me that he's coming home tomorrow. He's going to collect a few things, and then he's going on another cruise with her, this time to the Mediterranean."

"Great," Brad said. "I'll have a little word with him. If you see him, don't tell him that I'm looking for him. I'll phone you tomorrow."

*

Nicole suddenly realised what was the most important thing in her life. It was what she needed more than anything else. It was a shock to her senses. She had enjoyed seeing the two men burn to death and hoped that they suffered. What she needed was to make the people who had raped her suffer. It was like the scales of justice. They needed to suffer as much, if not more, than she had suffered. She wanted them to suffer and die.

Up until the car chase, she had wanted the men who had raped her to be arrested, but not anymore. She now wanted them to die, but it was more than that. It would not satisfy her if they just died. She would feel cheated. She wanted to kill them. She had to kill them. She had to pull the trigger and watch them die. The thought of killing them excited her, and she felt almost euphoric. For the first time since the rape, she was looking forward to doing something. For the first time, she saw a light at the end of her tunnel of despair. For the first time, she felt that she was now on the mend, and it was all thanks to Brad. Without his help, she would still be wallowing in her grief and pain.

There was a definite change in her. It was a subtle, small change, but it was there. She could feel it growing. She had a swim and then sat listening to her CDs. She was still ill and needed her tablets, but she was convinced that she had found the key to her recovery. Killing the rapists was the key.

She was playing her violin in the lounge when her parents came home. They looked amazed.

"I don't believe it," her mother said. "I never thought I'd see you play again. Are you going to resume your violin lessons?"

"I don't know. I might."

"You look like a million dollars, Nicole," her father said. "I think we'll celebrate."

"I would look at the Porsche first," Nicole said. "I took Brad out today, and I crashed it. It was only a small crash, but it dented the car."

"Did you drive?" her mother asked.

"Yes, and I enjoyed it."

Her mother kissed her on the cheek. "I'm so pleased. I was hoping that Brad would help you to start living again. He's such a nice lad."

"And don't worry about the car," her father said. "As long as you're not hurt, I don't care."

"Your Aunty Silvia's coming around later," her mother said. "Your cousin John will be bringing her. Do you feel up to meeting her?"

"Yes." Nicole quite liked Silvia, although she had no time for big-headed John. "It'll be nice to see her again."

Her father flopped into an armchair. "Travelling to and from work's killing me. I've found this house in Dorridge. It's perfect. Your mother likes it. Do you feel up to seeing it? I won't buy it if you don't like it."

"I'm going to buy a new car tomorrow," Nicole said. "If you give me the address, I'll drive over and have a look."

"What about my car?" her mother shouted from the kitchen.

"Sheryl still has it. If you have it back, they won't be able to get about, and they've been good to me."

"That's true," her mother said. "Your dad can buy me another car. Do you want a cup of tea?"

"Yes, please." Nicole sat down by her father. "Brad wants to see you about that job tomorrow. He's very keen."

"Good." Her father was looking at the television magazine. "He can start as soon as he likes." He put the magazine down and switched on the television. "I've got some literature for him to read."

"I feel nervous when I go out," she said. She lowered her voice so that her mother could not hear. "Are you still a member of the gun club?"

"Yes. I don't go so often now. Why do you ask?"

"I need a gun."

He stared at her for a few seconds. "Why?"

"I'll feel safer if I have a gun."

"I know what you mean." He looked around to check that her mother was not listening. "After you were raped, I got a couple of guns for protection. I've got a dozen legal guns and a shotgun, but they're locked up at the club. The two guns I bought are illegal. The police don't allow people to have guns in their homes. You could get into trouble carrying a gun."

"I would rather go to prison than be raped again."

He nodded. "I would as well. If you're ever attacked, blow their bleeding heads off."

"I will. Does that mean you will give me the guns?"

"Yes, but you'll only need one gun."

"Brad needs a gun as well."

Her father frowned. "Why does Brad need a gun?"

"Brad will be with me, and if I'm attacked, he will be able to help me if he has a gun. It's very important that we both have a gun."

He blew out his cheeks. "Okay. I'll give you the guns, but don't tell your mother."

"I won't. I also want two bulletproof vests."

Her father stared at her for a few seconds with his mouth open. "Good God. Are you that frightened?"

"Yes. I now know how bad the world is, and I panic every time I go out. Brad is helping me to get back into life, and I can only do it if I know I can protect myself and fight back. I don't ever intend to get raped again."

"I can understand how you feel." He went to pat her knee but thought better of it. He was obviously conscious of how she felt about being touched by a man. "I'll do anything to make you well again, but don't ever tell anyone that I gave you the guns. If the police find the guns and the vests, you'll have to say that you took the vests out of my study without asking and that you found the guns."

"I will," she promised.

*

Brad was knackered and just wanted sex and an early night. Tina had different ideas. She wanted him to take her to The Sack of Potatoes and make up the numbers for a quiz contest organised by the university. "I'm almost brain-dead," he said. "I'm no good at quizzes."

"It's all right," Tina said. "As long as you buy me a drink and pay the four-pound admission fee. I'm broke."

She was providing him with free sex and accommodation, so he could not refuse. They met the other four members of their quiz team at the pub, had a drink and then walked over the road to the university. The questions they were asked were way above his head, and he only knew those on sport. It did not matter, though. They had a bloke nicknamed Brains on their team, and he knew most of the answers. They tied with another team for first place.

"Oh, no," Tina said.

"What's wrong?" Brad asked. "With Brains here, we can't lose."

"You don't understand," Tina said. "Each team can pick from the other team who they want to answer the questions in the knockout decider. We're going to pick Sally. She only knows about music, geography and history. But they are bound to pick you, and you only know about sport. We could have won a hundred quid."

"Oh. I see what you mean," Brad said. He resented the implication that he was thick.

The other team picked him to answer the questions, and his team picked Sally. He felt very self-conscious with dozens of university students looking at him. He was bound to make a fool of himself. They were to be asked the same questions and had to write down the answers. Neither of them knew the answers to the first five questions. Everyone was laughing at them. The next subject was biology.

"Name the shell-like bone in the ear," the question master asked.

"The funny bone," someone shouted.

Sally shook her head. "I haven't a clue," she said. She was a dumb blonde and was definitely not a university student.

"This could go on all night," someone else shouted.

"Be quiet," the question master shouted.

Brad could not believe it. He knew the answer. It was the only thing about the body that he knew. "The cochlea," he said.

"Correct," the question master said, and everyone cheered.

Brad shared the hundred-pound prize money with the other members of his team, and they patted him on the back.

"Well done," Tina said. "How did you know it was called the cochlea?"

He shrugged. "I just did. I'm not completely thick." He did not intend to tell her that he only knew the answer because of a dirty joke he had been told at school.

He had too much to drink, and it took longer than normal to climax when he had sex with Tina that night, and she screamed five times. It was deafening and must have been heard by the whole neighbourhood. He fell asleep with a smile on his face.

Chapter Fourteen

Nicole woke up and lay staring at her bedroom ceiling. It was not possible. It was light, so it must be morning. She looked at the clock. It was six-thirty. She smiled. She had not had a nightmare. Why? Was it something to do with the men dying? She was still half asleep. She sat up. No. It was probably because she was going after the men who had raped her.

The sleep began to leave her mind, and her thoughts became clear. What was she thinking? It had nothing to do with going after the rapists. It was because she had found the key to her illness. She no longer wanted the rapists to go to prison. She had not had her nightmare because she was going to kill all five of the bastards who had made a mess of her life. She now had a reason to live.

She climbed out of bed, slipped off her nightdress and walked into the en-suite shower. She intended to shoot them and watch them die. She switched on the shower. She might then be able to get her life back and begin living again.

*

The tune on his mobile phone woke him up. Brad picked up the phone. Who the fuck was calling him so early? "Yes?"

"It's Nicole. Did I wake you?"

"Yes. Do you know what time it is?"

"Yes. It's nearly ten o'clock."

"Is it?" He looked at his watch. It was nine forty-five. "I thought it was earlier than that. What do you want?"

"I've bought a new car. I took a taxi to a local dealer and snapped up one of his bargains. Are you coming over, or do you want me to pick you up?"

"I'm supposed to be seeing Wayne," he said. Tina woke up and began to massage his limp penis.

"I can take you to see Wayne," Nicole said.

"What did your parents say about the Porsche?"

"Nothing. It's insured, and they're glad to see me getting out and doing things. Are you coming for breakfast, or do you want me to pick you up?"

He was starving, and Wayne could wait. "I could do with breakfast and a shower. I'll be there in forty-five minutes."

"Make that sixty-five minutes," Tina whispered as she squeezed his erect penis.

"Okay," Nicole said. "Bye."

*

Nicole ended the call and put the phone down. She had heard what Tina had said, and even though she had no intention of having sex with Brad, she felt a pang of jealousy.

*

It was twelve o'clock when Brad sat down to breakfast in Nicole's kitchen and five past twelve when he had eaten it. "That's better," he said. "I needed that."

Nicole placed a cup of tea in front of him and put his plate into the dishwasher. "It's a wonder you don't get indigestion. You eat like a wild animal, as if you think someone will take the food away from you. I'm sure you don't chew your food."

"Don't nag. I only eat fast when I'm starving." He watched her wipe the table. She looked different somehow. "You seem better today."

"I am. You will never guess what happened."

"What?"

"Have a guess."

He blew out his cheeks. "It must be something good." He then realised what was different about her. It was her eyes. Her eyes were no longer sad and tired. They now look like they did before she became ill. "You didn't wet the bed."

"Close. Have another guess."

What could have happened that would have been wonderful? He suddenly realised what it was. "You didn't have a nightmare?"

"Correct. I'll be able to cope better if I can get a good night's sleep. I'm going to try to do without the sleeping tablets." She looked him up and down. He had worn the same jeans and sweater for a week. "Don't you ever change your clothes?"

"I'd like to, but they're hanging up in my bedroom. I intended to get them when I went to see Tim, but I forgot." He suddenly became conscious of his attire. "I need to get some underpants, socks and shirts, but I'm not rolling in cash."

"You can borrow a shirt and a jumper from my dad, and I'll buy you some underpants and socks," she said. "We can get them on the way to Birmingham."

He stood up. "I'll have a quick shower if it's all right?"

"You don't have to ask. You almost live here."

He helped himself to a shirt and a jumper from her father's wardrobe and had a shower. He would have to go back to his house and get all of his clothes. His jeans were filthy, and his trainers were falling to bits.

Nicole drove them to Birmingham in her new car, a three-year-old Ford. She preferred it to the Porsche, and it would be less conspicuous when they went back to Handsworth. They drove in silence. She turned on the radio. Brad looked worried. She pulled up outside the University.

"Why are we stopping here?" he asked.

"I'm going to pick up your disguise. I've arranged to meet Emma, a friend of Sheryl's."

She walked across the car park and into the Halls of Residence. She felt a bit panicky. She always did when she was alone and away from her house. The taxi drive this morning to get her car had been an ordeal. She had needed to take a tablet and drink a can of lager before she had been able to get into the taxi. Even though she felt a little better in herself, it was going to take a long time for her to make a full recovery.

She collected a box from Emma and returned to the car. It was silly how a small walk on her own terrified her. It was probably some form of agoraphobia. She climbed into the car and handed him the box. She felt better inside the car.

He opened the box. It contained a beard, a moustache, glasses and a wig. He tried them on. The moustache looked ridiculous. The beard looked even worse. He settled for the long-haired wig and the glasses. "What do you think?"

She glanced at him as she drove along. He looked very different. "No one will recognise you, that's for sure. Don't you fancy the beard?"

"No. It looks ridiculous, and it itches."

On their way to Wayne's house, he saw Wayne walking along. He was wearing a hat pulled over his face, but Brad would know him anywhere. "It's Wayne," he said. "Pull over." She stopped the car, and Brad climbed out.

Wayne stopped and stared at him. He looked frightened. "What do you want?"

"To talk to you, you prat," Brad said.

"Fucking hell, Brad," Wayne said. "You scared the shit out of me. I didn't recognise you. Why the disguise?"

"Get inside the car," Brad said. "We can't talk here."

They both climbed into the back of the car.

Brad felt like breaking his neck. "What the fuck are you playing at?"

"What do you mean?" Wayne asked.

"You killed two blokes and then left me to take the rap," Brad said.

Wayne looked shocked. "Who said I killed two blokes?"

"Don't fuck with me," Brad said. "I know you did it. What I don't know is why?"

"I haven't killed anybody," Wayne insisted.

Brad was beginning to lose his temper. "Any more crap out of you, and I'll smash your fucking face in."

Wayne stared at him for a few seconds and then sighed. "I had to. They were going to kill me. Have you told the cops?"

"No, but I'm going to. I want them off my back." He decided not to tell Wayne that the gang had tried to kill him twice. "I want you to tell the police that you killed them."

"No way," Wayne said. "Do you think I'm fucking mad?"

"If you don't see the cops today, I'm going to see them," Brad said. "And they'll pick you up in five minutes. But before I go to the cops, I'll be kicking the shit out of you."

Wayne took out a packet of cigarettes and offered one to Brad and Nicole. "Is this your girl?"

"Yes," Brad said. He lit the cigarettes. "She knows everything and can be trusted."

She was pleased that Brad felt he could trust her. She would not trust Wayne an inch.

"What do I tell the police?" Wayne asked.

"Tell them the truth," Brad said. "Or at least some of it. Tell them that the thugs thought that you were muscling in on their business and tried to kill you, and that, with the help of your trained dog, you disarmed them and shot them. If you killed them in self-defence, you won't do time."

"What you said is exactly what happened," Wayne said. "I'm not too worried about the cops; it's this gang that frightens me. I had two minders. They weren't frightened of anybody, but when I had trouble with this gang, they fucked off and left me."

"I'll drop you off at the police station," Brad said.

"Hang on," Wayne said. "I didn't say I would do it."

Brad was at the point of losing his temper. All the trouble he was in was down to Wayne. "If you don't, I'll kick the shit out of you and take you myself. Either way, you're going to the cop shop."

"Let me think," Wayne said.

They sat smoking for a few minutes.

Nicole was enjoying herself. Her life had changed from being very boring to being dangerous and exciting. She looked at Brad through the rear-view mirror. He looked intelligent in glasses.

"Okay," Wayne said. "I don't have any fucking choice, and I thought you were my mate."

"This is not down to me," Brad said. "You got involved in drugs, and it was you who involved me in your problems."

They dropped a miserable-looking Wayne outside Steel House Lane police station and watched him walk in the door. They then drove to the end of the road and watched the door in case he came out again. After ten minutes, they drove off.

"I don't trust him," Nicole said, "and I can't see him confessing to anything."

"You could be right, but I've got no choice."

She looked at her watch. "I'm going out with the girls tonight, and I need to get my hair done. I've got an appointment at the hairdresser's at three-thirty. Are you coming back with me, or do you want me to drop you off somewhere?"

"I thought I was seeing your father," he said.

"Oh. I forgot to tell you. My father's going out for a meal. He said that he'll see you over the weekend. I've asked him to get me two handguns and two bulletproof vests."

"And what did he say?"

"He said that he would get them for me."

Brad was shocked. "How is he going to get two handguns?"

"He's been a member of a gun club since he was a teenager. When handguns were made illegal, many of the men at the gun club hid their guns. Some of them are very valuable. My dad has two illegal guns and a shotgun. He also knows the man who owns the gun shop in Solihull, so he can get all the ammunition he needs."

"Great," he said. "I'll feel better with a gun."

"If we're caught with the guns, we'll have to say that we found them," she said. "I don't want my father getting into trouble."

"The police won't believe we found them," he said. "If we're caught, say I bought them from a man in a pub. It sounds more believable. You can drop me here. I'll see you tomorrow."

She dropped him off and drove home. It was nerve-racking driving on her own, but she preferred it to taking a taxi. Everything she did on her own was an ordeal, even going to the hairdresser, but if she wanted to get better, she needed to push herself.

As soon as she drove into the drive of her house, she began to relax. The men who had raped her and all but destroyed her life were going to pay in full for what they had done. She was determined to kill them and would overcome any obstacle to do it.

*

Brad was walking towards the bus stop when his mobile phone rang. He took it out of his pocket. "Yes?"

"It's Dan. I'm at the snooker hall. I've got some bad news."

"What bad news?" Brad asked. "What's happened?"

"I'll put Carl on," Dan said.

"Hi, Brad," Carl said. "I've just been speaking to your next-door neighbour. He told me that someone beat up your parents and Tim, and they went to Heartlands Hospital."

Brad stopped walking and stared into the distance. "How bad are they?"

"I don't know. Your dad drove them to the hospital, so he can't be too badly injured. I think Tim has a broken arm."

"Are they at the hospital now?" Brad asked.

"No. They're back home."

"Do you know who did it?" Brad asked.

"Yes," Carl said. "Two blacks. What are you going to do?"

"I don't know yet. Are you sure it was two blacks?"

"Yes. I thought you killed the two blacks who shot you?"

"I did. It's obviously two different men."

"Did you see Wayne?" Carl asked.

"Yes. I took him to the cop shop. He's going to tell them that he shot the blacks."

"Not if I know Wayne," Carl said. "He wouldn't admit to anything. What made him go? Did you threaten him?"

"Yes. I told him I would kill him if he didn't go."

Carl laughed. "I now understand why he went."

He said goodbye to Carl and phoned his father, who now had Brad's old phone. The number was unobtainable. He did not have a clue where his Uncle John lived or his phone number, so he would not be able to contact his family.

He began to walk towards Tina's flat. The gang must have found out where his family was living, or maybe his family had moved back home. If they had moved back home, he would be able to visit them. He stopped walking and chewed his lip. No. It would be too risky. He continued walking. The gang and the police could be watching his house.

The gang was probably pissed off because he had killed the two men. They were going to be even more pissed off when he went to see them again. He could not wait to get his hands on a gun. What he could not understand was why the gang had not severely hurt his family. He would have expected them to have done more than just rough them up. Before he did anything, he would have to make sure that his family were safe and could not be traced.

While eating fish and chips in Tina's flat that evening, a news item on the television cheered him up. A man was helping the police with their enquiries concerning the shooting of two men at the rear of a snooker hall in Ladywood. If Wayne were convicted of the murders, the gang and the police would stop looking for him. He got drunk that night, and Tina screamed three times.

Chapter Fifteen

Nicole sang as she showered. It was the first time she had sung since her rape ordeal. She stared at her reflection in the full-length mirror. She had lost weight, and her ribs stuck out, although she still had large breasts. In time, she might even have sex. It would please Brad if she did. Since the rape, she had lost all sexual feelings and had not even masturbated.

She towelled herself down and tried to analyse how she felt and what had changed in her. Something had changed, and it was more mental than physical. Something had changed in her mind, something deep in her subconscious, and to say that a key had unlocked something was probably an oversimplification.

Since the rape, she had suffered from an extremely painful worry that stuck in her mind like a thorn. It was always there, and it clung to her thoughts. When she thought of doing something or going somewhere, this thing would attack her thoughts and corrode and destroy them, and she would begin to feel depressed. Everything would then turn grey, and she would lose interest.

That thing; that thorn, had gone, and it went the moment she decided to kill the men who had raped her. It was as if the thought of killing them had acted like tweezers, plucking the thorn out of her mind. Her thoughts were now clear and fresh, and she did not get depressed when she thought of doing something.

She began to sing again. She still had anxiety and would have a panic attack if she pushed herself too hard. She needed alcohol and her tablets, but with a clear mind and no nightmares, she felt more optimistic about the future. In time, she hoped to stop taking her tablets and start to live again. She dressed and cooked herself a huge breakfast.

Her mother walked into the kitchen. "Is Brad here?" she asked.

"No. He'll be here later on."

Her mother pointed to the breakfast. "Who have you cooked that for?"

"For me. I'm starving." She sat down and began to eat.

Her mother sat down facing her. "If you eat all of that, I'll know you're on the mend."

Nicole finished her breakfast, except for one sausage and drank her tea. "I think I am on the mend, and it's all down to Brad."

Her mother smiled. "Have you kissed him yet?"

"No. I still can't bear to be touched." She picked up her violin. "I think I'll play my violin in my bedroom."

*

Brad bent Tina over the bed and made her scream twice, and then phoned the snooker hall. The manager answered and told him that it was too early for

Carl or Dan. Brad said that he would phone back later. He sat on the bed and watched Tina putting on her makeup. He felt depressed. He missed playing snooker and was worried about his family. He picked up his phone and phoned Nicole. The number was unobtainable. He phoned Nicol's house phone.

"Yes?" Nicole's mother said.

"Hello, Pat. It's Brad. Is Nicole there?"

"Hello, Brad. Yes. She's playing her violin in her room, and I don't want to disturb her. What do you want?"

"I just wanted to know if it's all right for me to come over and have a word with Andy?"

"Yes. Andy's expecting you. Nicole will also want to see you."

"Great. I'll be there in about an hour."

He bought a new sweater and had breakfast in a cafe. If Nicole was playing her violin, she must be feeling good. She was an unusual woman. She was terrified of being alone, but was unmoved by the death of two men. And now that he thought about it, all women were unusual.

*

Her mother walked into Nicole's bedroom. "I didn't want to interrupt you while you were playing your violin. How are you feeling? Did playing the violin help?"

"Yes." Nicole switched her phone back on and put it into her bag. "I'm going to phone Lucinda Evens and resume my lessons."

"Oh, that is good news," her mother said. "I've been waiting for you to stop playing so that I could tell you that Brad phoned. He said that he would be here in about an hour." She looked at her watch. "And that was just over an hour ago."

The doorbell rang. "That must be him," Nicole said.

"I'll get it," her father shouted from the hall.

Nicole's father opened the door. "Come in, Brad. I hear you want a job?"

"Yes." Brad stepped into the hall. "I like the idea of selling security gadgets. It sounds very interesting."

Nicole's father closed the door. "It is interesting. I've got some literature and a few gadgets in my study for you to look at."

Nicole walked down the stairs. "I want to cook Brad breakfast first before you interrogate him."

"I've just had breakfast," Brad said. He did not want Nicole's parents to know that he used their house as a cafe.

"Then come into my study, both of you," Nicole's father said. "I've got things to show you, and I've got a golfing appointment in two hours."

"I'll get two cans of lager, and I'll join you," Nicole said.

Nicole walked into the kitchen and took two cans of lager out of the fridge. She walked out of the kitchen and into her father's study.

"I've got a driving licence, but I've never been able to afford a car," Brad was saying.

"That's no problem," her father said. "You'll get a car with the job, although it'll probably take a couple of weeks. My partner, Tom, likes to be involved in everything."

She handed Brad a can of lager and sat down. Her father sounded so professional.

Brad had a drink and smiled at Nicole. "This sounds like a job of a lifetime."

"It is." Nicole's father handed him a huge folder. "This is what we sell. Don't worry about the electrics. All you need to know is what we sell and what it does, but not how it works. The stuff's made in America, and we have a franchise to sell it. Some of it is space-age stuff, and we only sell to the rich and the famous, but don't worry about that. You'll only be selling the more mundane products at first." He took a pen out of his briefcase. "Such as this."

"What is it?" she asked. "It looks like a pen."

"It's a listening device," her father said. "Don't ask me how it works. I only sell them." He stood up. "Let's go into the back garden, and I'll show you what it can do."

Brad followed them into the back garden. Nicole was wearing a tight skirt, and her bum cheeks moved as she walked. She had lost weight, but she still had a mind-blowing shape. If only she were well enough to have sex. He could do things to that bum.

"Go to the bottom of the garden, Brad," Nicole's father said. "To the other side of the apple trees."

Brad jogged across the lawn.

"Put this in your ear," her father said to Nicole. "It's designed to look like a hearing aid. You won't believe what this little pen can do. It's like magic."

Brad stopped and turned around. He was about a hundred metres away. "What do I do?" he shouted.

"Just a minute," Nicole's father shouted.

"Twist the top of the pen and point it at Brad," her father said.

"Say something in a whisper," Nicole's father shouted to Brad.

"I would love to feel your tits," Brad whispered.

She smiled. She had heard him as clearly as if he had been standing next to her. "Don't be rude," she shouted.

"What did he say?" her father asked.

"I'd rather not say. It was rude."

"You can come back now," Nicole's father shouted.

Brad walked back towards them. There was no way that she could have heard what he had whispered, but she must have. That gadget could come in handy.

She was very impressed. "But what would have happened if Brad had shouted?"

"Nothing," her father said. "What you hear is actually a recording that is played back almost instantaneously, and if the sound goes above a certain decibel, the sound is reduced so that it always sounds the same. It works up to a distance of two hundred metres if there isn't too much wind or background noise. You can also play back the last three minutes by pressing the top." He took the earpiece from her, put it into his ear and pressed the top of the pen. He smiled. "It was rude, wasn't it?"

Brad walked up to them. "Did you hear what I said?" he asked.

"Yes," she said. "It's a brilliant little gadget." She turned to her father. "Could we borrow it?"

"Yes," her father said. "It's a demonstration model for Brad. Let's go inside. I've got something else for you."

They followed Nicole's father back to his study.

Brad was hoping that the something else was the guns. "When will I know when I've got the job?"

"You've already got the job," Nicole's father said. "Let me have a CV and fill in the application form. You can start next week."

When they were in the study, Nicole's father locked the door. "I don't like doing this," he said. "If the police search you or your car and find the guns, you'll get in trouble. I suggest that you always wipe them after touching them. You can then claim that they are not yours." He opened a drawer, took out two packages and handed one to Nicole and one to Brad. "They're very dangerous, so don't fool around with them."

Nicole opened the package. The gun was in a little holster. "How does it work?"

"I'll show you," her father said.

They spent the next ten minutes loading and unloading the guns. Brad's gun looked very powerful. "We might need more ammunition?" Brad said.

Nicole's father looked concerned. "Why would you want more ammunition?"

The question stumped Brad, but for only a few seconds. "I was hoping to go into the country and practice shooting the gun."

"It would be too risky," Nicole's father said. "I'm hoping that you'll never use the guns. You have one full clip of fifteen bullets. Nicole's clip holds seven bullets. If you do need more ammunition, let me know. I would put on the shoulder holster, Brad, and always check that the safety catch is on before handling it."

"I will." Brad put on the shoulder holster. It fitted under his coat and felt good.

"Do I have to carry mine in my handbag?" she asked.

"Yes," her father said. "You walk around half-naked, and if you have it on your person, it will stand out." He handed them two parcels. "These are the bulletproof vests. They're demonstration models." He looked at his watch. "I'll have to be off." He unlocked the door. "And remember the golden rule: if the police question you about anything, deny it."

"We already know that rule," Brad said. "And thanks for helping us, and thanks for the job."

"It's a pleasure," Nicole's father said. "It would help if you study what's in the folder."

"I will," Brad said.

Nicole's father left to play golf, and Brad and Nicole sat on the patio. This time, Nicole sat next to him on the swinging seat.

"Are you sure this seat is strong enough?" he asked. "You do have a big bum."

She dug him in the ribs with her elbow. "You cheeky bugger."

He smiled and took out his cigarettes. She had actually touched him. Things were taking a turn for the better.

"I feel better with a gun," she said. "It'll make killing them easy."

"It will not be easy," he said. "The guns just make it possible. They're very dangerous men." He then remembered his family. "The drug gang roughed up my family again."

She turned and stared at him. "Your mother as well?"

"Yes."

"Are they hurt?" she asked.

"Yes." He offered her a cigarette. "They went to hospital. I don't think they're too badly hurt. I wish I could contact them."

"Why can't you phone them?" she asked.

"There's no phone at home, and none of them has a mobile phone. Dad has my old phone, but I don't think it's switched on. Tim said he was getting a phone, but I don't know the number. There is a chance they might be living at my Uncle John's, but I don't have his number."

"What are you going to do?" she asked."

"I've asked Carl and Dan to see if they can find out how they are."

They sat smoking.

She felt so angry. The thugs who were after Brad were obviously very dangerous if they resorted to beating up women, and if they were the same men who had raped her, she knew just how dangerous they were.

He took out his mobile phone. "I'll give Dan a call." He phoned the snooker hall. The manager answered and told him that Carl and Dan had not been in. Brad thanked him and put the phone into his pocket. "He's not there. I'll phone later."

"When are we going to Handsworth again?" she asked.

"I'm not sure." He was worried about his family and wanted to make sure they were safe before he did anything. "I want to check on my family first."

Brad spent an hour studying the contents of the folder and then began to eat the meal she had cooked for him. While he ate the meal, she played her violin. She was very talented. He could not relax. He would feel better when he had seen his family.

At five o'clock, after sitting on the patio with Nicole for a couple of hours, he stood up. "I'm leaving now."

She stood up. "Are you coming back tomorrow?"

"It's Sunday," he said. "What will your parents think? I don't want to outstay my welcome."

"Don't be silly. They don't mind. Get here early, and I'll cook you breakfast."

He left, and she went for a swim. She had not told Brad that she intended to kill the men who had raped her. He would probably think that she was not capable of such a manly action. He was going to be in for a surprise, and so were the men who had raped her.

Sheryl, Linda and Angela arrived at seven as Nicole was drying her hair in her bedroom. Her mother let them in and sent them upstairs. Linda jumped onto Nicole's bed. "Are you coming out with us on a regular basis?" Linda asked Nicole.

"Yes. I enjoyed myself." They had been to a karaoke evening and had sung together.

"We need to practice for next week," Angela said. "Can we have a drink to get us in the mood?"

"Yes," Nicole said. "Get one out of the fridge."

"We're so glad you're on the mend, Nicole," Sheryl said. "Is it because Brad's bonking you?"

Linda tickled Nicole. "I bet you've been at it like rabbits."

"We have not," Nicole said. "We're just friends."

"I don't believe that for one second," Angela said. "He's here nearly every day."

"I'm not ready for anything like that." Nicole put her hairdryer away and opened a can of lager. "I'm getting better, but I still can't bear a man to touch me."

"I'm the same," Linda said.

They laughed.

"You can't wait for them to touch you," Sheryl said. "They don't call you Lusty Linda for nothing."

It lifted Nicole's spirits to be with her friends. When they began to practise singing, she was enjoying herself so much she forgot all about pain, rape and mental anguish.

*

Brad phoned the snooker Hall three times, but his mates were not there. It would help if they had a mobile phone. His priority was to clear things with the police so that he could visit his family. It was a nightmare hiding from gun-crazy blacks and the police. He spent the evening in The Sack of Potatoes with Tina and her university friends. The lager did not lift his spirits. When they returned to Tina's flat, he was not in the mood for sex, and Tina only screamed once.

Chapter Sixteen

At ten o'clock in the morning, Brad caught the bus to Nicole's house. It was a long, boring journey. When he arrived, she cooked him a large breakfast. Bohemian Rhapsody was reverberating around the kitchen, and she was dancing in the lounge. He watched her as he ate. She seemed like a different person. Not quite what she used to be, but she was getting there. "Did you have a nightmare last night?" he asked.

"No." She walked into the kitchen and stared at him. "What's wrong? You're not your usual cocky self. Are you still worried about your family?"

"Yes." He put the last piece of sausage into his mouth and pushed the plate away. "I was not really interested in going after the gang after the two blacks had died. I felt that I had taken my revenge. I was just helping you. It's different now. This time, they hurt my mother."

"Didn't your family have police protection?"

"No." He offered her a cigarette. "They were living at my uncle's. The blacks must have found out where they were living. It seems that these blacks are clever bastards."

She lit a cigarette. "What are you going to do?"

"I want to go to see the police and then see my family. It's this gang that's worrying me. Do you fancy a ride?"

"Yes. I'll get my coat."

They climbed into her car, and she drove following his directions. She could sense that he was worried, but she did not know what to say to cheer him up. It was probably how he had felt about her when she had been ill. Had been? What was she thinking? She was still ill, although she was now on the mend.

They pulled up outside the snooker hall, and he checked his disguise in the mirror. "You can wait here if you like?"

"No. I'll come in with you." She did not want to be left on her own, especially in a rough area.

She followed him into the snooker hall. It was just like a large shed full of snooker tables. It was a depressing place and had not been decorated for years. They walked up to a bar that served drinks and sandwiches. Brad stood next to two men about his age. The two men were talking to each other. One of them turned to look at Brad. "Fucking hell," the man said. "I didn't recognise you."

"Keep your voice down, Dan," Brad said. He looked about. There were about thirty people in the snooker hall. "Are the men who are after me here?"

"No," Dan said. "They were here a short time ago. They said that they're not interested in you anymore."

Brad sat down. "A likely story. Why aren't they interested in me?"

"They didn't say," Dan said.

They might be claiming to have forgotten about him, but Brad had not forgotten about them. "This is Nicole. Dan and Carl."

They nodded and smiled at each other.

Nicole sat down next to Brad. "If the men are not looking for you, you can go and see your family," she said.

"Yes," Brad said. "After I've been to see the police." He turned to Carl. "Have you been to see my family?"

"No," Carl said. "I phoned the hospital, but they wouldn't tell me a thing. I was going to pop round to your house this afternoon to see if they were there."

"What are you going to do about them hurting your family?" Dan asked Brad.

"Pay them a visit," Brad said.

"I would let sleeping dogs lie," Carl said. "They said that they're not interested in you anymore, and they're not the sort of people to mess with."

Brad stood up. "I think they are still interested in me. We're off. We'll see you later."

"Is this where you used to play snooker?" she asked as she followed him to the car.

"Yes."

"It's a bit rough," she said.

"Yes." He was only half-listening. He was worrying about his family.

She drove him to the police station. She was not sure it was a good idea. They could keep him in for days. They can do anything when conducting a murder investigation. She pulled up outside the police station. "Do you want me to come in with you?"

"No. It's best I go in on my own. I could be hours."

She did not want to wait alone. "I'll park in the university car park. I need to see my tutor. When you come out, give me a call. You have my mobile number."

"I will," he said.

It took him over an hour to give his statement to the police. He was then escorted to the back door of the police station by the policeman who had taken his statement. Brad was relieved. He had never trusted the police. They would pin anything on you if they could.

The policeman opened the back door. "I think I'd better put you straight," he said.

Brad lit a cigarette. "What about?"

"Wayne Turnbull did not confess," the policeman said. "He claims he didn't shoot the two men."

Brad felt angry. "The bastard. If Wayne said that he did not shoot the two men, why are you releasing me? You said that my prints were on the gun."

The policeman smiled. "Your prints were on the gun, but not on the trigger. We believe that your friend Wayne wiped the gun before putting it down where you would find it. He tried to set you up. He's a crafty bugger."

Brad felt confused. "I still don't understand. Where's Wayne?"

"Locked up," the policeman said. "He did not wipe the gun properly. He left one of his fingerprints on the gun, and it was half underneath one of your prints, and he's still claiming that he never touched the gun."

"So, I'm in the clear?" Brad asked.

"Yes. The witness, who saw you go down the side of the snooker hall, said that she heard what sounded like gunshots a short time before you came out of the snooker hall. You're in the clear, but we'll need you as a witness."

"Thank God for that," Brad said. "I'll be a witness, all right. I hope that bastard Wayne gets twenty years."

Brad walked out of the police station. If it had not been for that one fingerprint, he would be going down instead of Wayne. The fucking bastard. He had deliberately left the gun where he would find it. He had probably watched him pick it up.

He phoned Nicole. "I'm outside the police station," he said.

"I'll be there in five minutes," she said.

A short time later, she pulled up next to him, and he climbed into the car.

"What happened?" she asked. "You've been ages. I've been so worried."

"I'm in the clear. We can now go and see my family."

She drove off. "Tell me what happened."

He told her briefly what had happened. As he talked, he was thinking about his family. If the thugs had hurt them, he would be going after them. He would wear his disguise, and there was no way they would recognise him. They pulled up outside his house. His Aunty Mary's car was parked in the drive. She was a cantankerous cow.

"Shall I come in?" she asked.

"Yes. I just want to find out how they are. They'll be pleased to know that the thugs won't be coming back." At least, he hoped not.

As soon as he walked into the kitchen, Brad knew that something was wrong. His father was sitting in a chair with his head in his hands, crying. It was the first time he had seen his father cry. Tim, who had a black eye, was standing next to him. "What's happened?" Brad asked. "Where's Mum?"

Aunty Mary walked into the kitchen. "Oh, it's you," she said. "My sister, your mother, passed away at one o'clock this morning."

Brad felt a shock wave surge through his body as if he had been electrocuted. His legs went weak, and he sat down. He had not expected anything like this.

Nicole was shocked. She put her hand on Brad's shoulder. His mother had been such a nice person.

"Where were you?" Aunty Mary asked Brad. "We had no way of contacting you."

"What happened?" Brad asked. He felt confused.

"It was the same black thugs," Tim said. "They surprised us."

"And it's all your fault," Aunty Mary said to Brad. "Them thugs would not have hurt your family if it wasn't for you. You were always causing trouble."

"Shut up," Brad shouted. He looked at his father. "What happened, Dad?"

"I'll not have you shouting at me," Aunty Mary said

"Then fuck off," Brad said.

"I think you'd better go, Mary," Brad's father said. "Thanks for your help. I'll phone you when I've sorted out the funeral arrangements."

Aunty Mary tut-tutted and walked out of the room.

Nicole did not like Mary. This was not the time to have a go at Brad.

Brad took out his cigarettes. "Did they beat Mum up?"

"No," his father said. "They kicked the back door in, punched Tim and knocked him out, and your mum fainted. They then roughed me up."

"The bastards," Brad said. "Did you get a look at them?"

"Yes," his father said. "They're nasty bastards. Are you going after them?"

Brad nodded.

"I would if I were younger," his father said. "They are both West Indian and both over six feet tall. One has a twisted little finger. I noticed it when he shoved a knife in my face. The other one has what looks like a tattoo of a spider's web behind his right ear. They both have shaven heads." His father stared at Brad for a few seconds. He then put on his glasses. "Is that a wig, and what's with the glasses?"

"It's a disguise," Brad said. He offered everyone a cigarette.

"You don't have to wear the disguise now," Nicole said.

"Oh, yes." Brad took off the wig and the glasses and handed them to Nicole. "The thugs won't be coming here again. They're not after me anymore."

"Thank God for that," Tim said. "They frightened me to death. I thought they were going to kill us. They somehow found out where we were living. We're moving to live somewhere else, and this time, we don't intend to tell anyone where we're going. Do you want a drink? Tea, coffee or lager?"

They all agreed on lager, and for a few minutes, no one spoke. They drank the lager and smoked.

Nicole felt sorry for Brad's father, whose eyes were red from crying. His cheek was grazed; he had not shaved and looked in a wretched state.

"Why did Mum die if she only fainted?" Brad asked. "Did she bump her head?"

"No," his father said. "I had a word with the doctor. She had another stroke. It was a big one. When we couldn't wake her up, we rushed her to the hospital, but she never regained consciousness and died last night."

Brad frowned. "What do you mean, another stroke?"

His father took a long drink of lager. "She'd already had two small strokes. She didn't want you to know. We told you that she was suffering from migraine."

"I should have been told," Brad said.

"It was your mother's decision," his father said. He began to cry. "God. What am I going to do? I can't live without your mum."

Brad stood up and put his arm around his father's shoulders. He did not know what to say. He looked at Tim. "You must be very careful from now on. Don't take any chances. Have you got a mobile phone?"

Tim nodded. "Dad's started using your old phone."

"Good," Brad said. "If you see or hear anything unusual, call the police and then phone me."

"Why?" Tim asked. "I thought they wouldn't be coming here again."

"I'm going after them," Brad said. "They might guess that it's me and come after you."

His father took his glasses off, wiped his eyes with the back of his hand and put them on again. "Are you really going after them?"

"Yes," Brad said. "Them two black bastards are as good as dead."

His father smiled. "Good. I thought you'd go after them. A chip off the old block." He looked up at Nicole. "It's good to see you again. I was expecting you two to get married."

"Things happen," Nicole said. This was not the time or place to explain what had happened to her.

"Yes," Brad's father said. "They certainly do."

Brad filled a suitcase with his clothes, exchanged mobile phone numbers, and was driven back to the centre of Birmingham by Nicole. It would not sink in that his mother was dead, and even though a stroke would be on the death certificate as the cause of death, he blamed the thugs. His mother could have lived for years if they had not frightened her. They were going to regret what they did.

"Do you want to drop these suitcases off at Tina's, or would you like to live at my house?" she asked. "We have three spare bedrooms."

He would rather live at Nicole's, but it would mean he would not be able to have sex with Tina if he did. "I don't know." He would be frustrated out of his mind if he did not have sex on a regular basis. "I don't want to upset Tina. What would your parents say?"

"I already mentioned it," she said. She was lying. "They said that you're welcome to stay as long as you like, and if you want sex, you can always pop in and see Tina."

"I wasn't thinking of sex," he said. He was. "Drop me at Tina's, and I'll have a word with her."

She pulled up outside Tina's flat, and she watched him walk through the front door. She did not want sex. She could not even be kissed, but she was jealous of him sleeping with Tina. Tina, of all people. Tina was well known for her threesomes.

*

Tina screamed as he placed his foot on the first tread of the staircase. He stopped. Tina was entertaining a bloke.

Tina's friend, Paulette, walked out of the kitchen. "Hi, Brad," she said. "That's the fourth scream."

"I'd better not go up if she's with a bloke," he said.

"She's with two blokes," Paulette said. "She likes to be done from both ends at the same time."

Tina screamed again. They smiled at each other.

"And I thought she loved me," he said.

"She does," Paulette said. "She loves all men."

"I think it's time for me to move on," Brad said. "Tell her that I'll be living somewhere else, but I'll give her a call when I feel like making her scream."

Paulette smiled. "I will. Tina's ever so nice, and I know she likes you. She's just sex mad."

He walked towards the door. "I'll ..."

Tina screamed again, and they both laughed.

"I saw you laughing when you came out of the door?" Nicole said when he had climbed into her car. "What was so funny?"

He decided not to tell her what had happened. "I cracked a joke to a friend of Tina's. I told her to tell Tina that I'll be staying at your house."

She started the car and drove off. "It won't upset me if you have sex with Tina, although I would always use a condom. She's very promiscuous, and you could catch something." She almost told him not to let her give him a blow job, but decided not to. "You're a free agent, and I understand how sexed-up men are."

"I don't discuss my sex life with anyone other than the person I have sex with," he said. "It's better that way."

Very diplomatic, she thought.

As she drove into her drive and parked next to her father's BMW, she remembered the holiday. She would have to phone Sheryl and see if it was still on. "Mum and Dad are home."

"Did you really ask them if I could stay?" he asked as he climbed out of her car with his suitcase.

"No, but it doesn't matter," she said. "They'll do anything for me."

"I had better put the case back in the car," he said. "It'll look bad if I walk in carrying a suitcase."

She grabbed his arm and pulled him towards the house. "Live dangerously." As she opened the door, she realised that she had held his arm for several seconds without panicking.

"I'll give you live dangerously," he said. "I feel I'm imposing." He followed her into the house, hid his suitcase under a table in the hall, and followed her into the lounge. Her parents were watching television. "Hello, Andy, hello, Pat," he said.

"Hello, Brad," Nicole's mother said.

"I've told Brad that he can live here for a while," Nicole said. "Will that be all right?"

"Yes," her mother said. She stood up. "I'll make us a cup of tea. "Are you together again?"

"No," Nicole said. "Just friends." She followed her mother into the kitchen. "I'll just give Sheryl a call."

"Sit down, Brad," Nicole's father said. "Do you fancy Nicole?" he whispered.

Brad sat down. "Yes."

"So, you might get back together?" Nicole's father asked.

"I doubt it. At least not for a long time. Nicole has gone completely off men."

Nicole's father nodded. "I know. I suppose it will take time. Did she tell you what happened?"

Brad nodded.

"It was a terrible business," Nicole's father said. "It knocked me and her mother about. We didn't know what to do." He smiled. "When I first met you, I told you, in so many words, not to jump into bed with Nicole. It's different now. The quicker you get her into bed, the better."

Brad smiled. "I'll do my best."

Nicole walked into the lounge. "The holiday's off."

"What holiday?" her father asked.

Nicole sat down. "I was going to have a long weekend in Paris with Linda, Angela and Sheryl, but Linda's had a row with her boyfriend, and she's too upset to go."

"That gives me an idea," her father said. He stood up and walked into the kitchen.

"When are we going after the thugs?" Nicole asked.

"Not for a few days. We need to let things calm down. If we do something straight away, they might suspect that I'm behind it."

She felt disappointed. "I suppose we could wait a week. Have you got a cigarette?"

He offered her a cigarette and took one himself. "We need to plan what we intend to do in detail. We can't just rush in there and start shooting. We need to use that pen and find out who the gang leaders are and where they live." He lit both cigarettes. "We'll then have to decide where and when to kill them." He whispered the words 'kill them.'

She stared at him. "I didn't realise you intended to kill them. I thought that it was just a figure of speech."

"It's the only way; otherwise, they'll keep coming after me. I'm hoping they won't recognise me and so won't know who's killing them."

She decided it was time to tell him what she intended to do. "I also want to kill the men who raped me."

It was understandable for her to want to kill them. "It could get dangerous." He took a drag on his cigarette and glanced at her. "Aren't you frightened? You could get injured or killed."

"No, not really. I'm more afraid of not killing them."

Nicole's father walked into the lounge. "Would it be all right if I had a week in Spain with your mother? We could do with a break."

She did not want to be left alone and began to panic until she realised that Brad would be living here. "Yes. Brad can look after me."

Her mother put her head around the door. "Are you sure?"

"Yes," Nicole said. "When are you going?"

"Tomorrow," her father said. "If we can get a flight. You can have Sheryl, Linda and Angela here if you want. You can even have a party."

"I would like to have a party," Nicole said.

Her father went into his study, and they sat smoking in silence.

It was obvious that Brad did not think that she was capable of killing someone. She would have to show him just how capable she was.

"Do you know what I want?" he asked.

She smiled. It was either sex or food. "No. What?"

"A swim."

"Then off you go," she said.

Chapter Seventeen

While Brad was having a swim, Nicole sat down on her bed and phoned Sheryl.

"Hello, Nicole," Sheryl said.

"How would you, Linda and Angela like to stay at my house for a week?" Nicole asked.

"Are your parents going away?"

"Yes. They're going on holiday tomorrow. You can bring your boyfriends if you like. We could have a howl."

"It sounds great," Sheryl said. "You sound more like the person you used to be. Are you doing it with Brad yet?"

"No. I'm a long way from that. When are you coming? We can do something different every day and have a party on Saturday."

"I'll phone the others," Sheryl said.

*

Brad swam slowly back and forth on his back. He would have to find out what it was that was stopping Nicole from touching a man and try to find a cure. If it were because of panic attacks, she could do what his father had done. Brad needed sex, and he did not feel like running to see Tina every few days. Nicole, who must be putting on weight, was getting her shape back. She had bent over this morning, and the sight of her shapely backside had blown his mind. He had a week to get her knickers off. The first thing they had to do was to talk to her.

Nicole walked into what she referred to as the pool room. "Are you still swimming?" she said. "You'll be all wrinkled."

"I am," he said. "My willy has shrivelled away. It's now only as big as a worm."

She decided to have a swim. "I don't want to know about little willies." She walked over to a cubicle. "I think I'll join you."

He was pleased. "When I went swimming with my mates in the winter in an open-air pool, it was so cold our willies almost disappeared." He suddenly realised that she might not want to talk about willies. "Did you phone Sheryl?"

"Yes. They're coming over this afternoon." She undressed and slipped on her swimsuit. It seemed to fit her better. She stepped on the scales. She could not believe it. She had put on six pounds. "I'm putting on weight. I think it's all the lager I'm drinking."

He lay on his back and watched her walk out of the cubicle and dive into the water. She had a gorgeous figure and huge breasts. "What stops you from touching a man?" There was no time like the present to try to sort out her problems.

She began to swim up and down. "What do you mean?"

"You know. Are you afraid of something?"

"No. It's not like that." They reached the opposite ends of the pool at the same time and then swam past each other. "I just get panicky, and if I let a man touch me or if I tried to have sex, I would have a panic attack. Even thinking about it makes me anxious."

He pulled himself out of the pool and sat on the side. "I might know a cure."

"What cure? Are you suggesting that I have sex with you? I can tell you now that it wouldn't work."

"No. I do want to have sex with you, but it's more complicated than that. When you've had your swim, I'll explain what I mean."

He dried himself, dressed and sat on the patio with a can of lager. It might not work, but it was worth a try.

She was intrigued to know what this cure was. Her therapist had not mentioned a cure. Her therapist had just advised her to do a little more every day, which is what she had been doing, and it seemed to be working. It was a very slow-moving cure and could take years. She could still not go out on her own or touch a man. She dressed and joined him on the patio. "Well, Dr Brad, what's this cure?"

"Did you get panic attacks before you were raped?" he asked.

"No." She sat down on the swinging seat and opened a can of lager. "I'm not a nervous person. I didn't know what a panic attack was until after I was raped. I was in the garden, and I suddenly panicked. I imagined the men who had raped me coming after me and raping me again. I had a full-scale panic attack. I thought I was dying. It was as bad as you can imagine."

They sat drinking for a while.

Her illness was very similar to his father's illness. Before his father became ill, he was a very brave man. "How often do you get these panic attacks?"

"At first, I had almost one a day. I was then given stronger tablets, and even though I sometimes feel panicky, I haven't had any more full-scale panic attacks. I live in dread of having a panic attack, and if I feel extra panicky, I take a tablet. Even the thought of having a panic attack makes me panic. In time, I hope to reduce the tablets and then stop them altogether."

"How often do you feel panicky?" he asked.

"About a hundred times a day. It drives me mad."

"What makes you panic?" he asked.

"Lots of things. What is this cure you mentioned?"

"My dad had a breakdown," he said. "He was working too hard and caught a strange illness. His temperature wouldn't go down, and he thought he was dying. About a month later, he began to have panic attacks."

"Does he still have them now?"

"No. He still has bad days, but he manages to deal with them. When he was ill and was having full-blown panic attacks almost every day, he found a way to stop them."

She sat on the edge of her seat. "What did he do?"

Brad emptied his can of lager and leaned back in his seat. "He was going to therapy sessions where mentally ill people sit in a circle and talk about their illnesses. It wasn't helping him one little bit. He then had a chat with this painter and decorator, who had a science degree, and the decorator told my dad what to do."

"You can't start taking advice from decorators," she said. "It could be dangerous, even if they do have a science degree."

"My dad's not daft. He had a word with the psychiatrist and told him what this decorator had said. The psychiatrist said that what the decorator had said was right and that it did work for some people. He told my dad to try it."

"What was it?" She was now very interested. She would do anything to get rid of her panic attacks.

"Do you panic for no reason?"

"What do you mean?"

"There are triggers that set off a panic attack, such as going into a lift or thinking about something that is not life-threatening. If you panic because a tiger's running towards you, it would be normal."

"I see what you mean," she said. "Yes. I panic if I'm alone, or if I get too close to a man, or if I think about what happened to me. My fears are irrational. I sometimes panic for no reason at all."

"Then it could work for you," he said.

"What could work?"

He then remembered something his father had said. "You can't try this cure if you've just become ill. You need to be recovering from whatever it was that made you ill."

"I am recovering from my illness. Will you tell me what this cure is?"

"That's what I'm doing. The first thing you have to do is to reprogram your amygdala."

She was beginning to feel confused. "What's an amygdala?"

"It's a primitive part of the brain that's been programmed to make you panic over silly things when you become ill. You need to reprogram it."

"How?"

"If you're panicking because you're on your own, you have to keep saying that being alone will not harm me."

"I already do that."

"Do you do it every day?"

"No. Not every day."

"You need to do it several times a day. You need to do it every time you panic over something silly."

"Is that the cure?" she asked.

"No. It's the first part of the cure."

"What's the second part of the cure?"

"It's very simple. You need to try to force yourself to have a panic attack."

She began to feel annoyed. She had expected him to say something sensible and profound. "What good will that do? I don't want to have a panic attack. I want to stop them."

"I'll try to explain," he said. "When we think, our thoughts travel around our brain on neural pathways, from one thought to the next. I'll prove it. What comes into your mind when I say five?" He waited a few seconds. "I bet it was six?"

She nodded. "Yes, but that's common sense."

"I know. It's how the brain works."

"How do you know all this?" she asked.

"I spent hours listening to that decorator talking with my dad. Where was I? Oh, yes. When you think of something that is a trigger, your thoughts travel around your brain along a panic pathway until it hits the panic button, and you have a panic attack."

"But what has that to do with trying to force a panic attack?"

"I'm trying to explain if you'll give me a chance. If you can move your thought off the panic pathway, the thought will get lost among the nerves and your memories, and your panicky feeling will go. If you imagine the panic thought travelling along the panic pathway, which is shaped like a twisted snake. If you force the panic thought to go in a straight line to the panic button, it will have to go off the panic pathway, and it will then get lost."

It sounded a bit complicated to her. "Did it work for your father?"

"Yes. He was sick of panicking over nothing. The more he appeased the panic, the worse he got. He told me that he was walking along the road one day, and he began to panic for no reason at all. He could feel the panicky feeling getting stronger as it moved along the panic pathway to the panic button. He stopped walking and tried to force the panic to go straight to the panic button. He shouted, 'Come on, you bastard. Come on. I'm not afraid of you. I'll wring your fucking neck.'"

"And what happened?" she asked.

"The panicky feeling disappeared. It vanished completely."

She took a drink of lager. It sounded too easy. "If it's that good, why doesn't everyone do it?"

"According to my father, it's very difficult to do, and as I said, you can only do it when you're recovering and not at the beginning of an illness. I'm not an expert. Talk it over with your doctor."

"I will." She looked at her watch. "She's coming this afternoon. Is your father cured?"

"No. He still carries a bottle of tablets around with him, and he still has bad days, although I don't think he's ever had a full panic attack since. He believes that it's the fear of panicking that makes you panic. You are, in effect, panicking about panicking."

He was right. She was more worried about having a panic attack than being raped. Now that she had a gun, she felt relatively safe, although she still felt panicky. "Have you ever had a panic attack?" she asked.

"No."

"They're terrifying." She shook her head. "You would have to be very brave to try to bring on a panic attack. I don't think I'm brave enough." She looked at her watch. "Do you want me to cook you something?"

"Yes. I'm starving to death."

"I've just enough time to cook you a meal before Miss Hastings arrives."

Her therapist, Miss Hastings, arrived at three o'clock, while Brad was eating his meal. She was on time as usual. Nicole showed her into her father's study.

"How are you feeling, Nicole?" Miss Hastings asked.

"A lot better." Nicole sat in her father's swivel chair and swivelled from side to side.

Miss Hastings sat down. "Have you had any nightmares?"

"No."

Miss Hastings smiled. "I am glad. Have you tried to be alone? You did say that you were going to go driving on your own."

"Yes. It's not easy, though. I still can't let a man touch me." She took out her cigarettes. "I would like to have sex. I have a boyfriend. The problem is, I begin to panic if I even think about having sex."

"What you need to do is take it step by step," Miss Hastings said. "First, try sitting close together. Then, hold hands. When you can hold his hand, you can then think of taking the next step. It will take time."

"My friend said that if I call the panic attack on and try to have a panic attack, it will go," Nicole said.

Miss Hastings chewed her lip. "I don't think you're ready for anything as drastic as that. Only a few people are brave enough to do it, and it's something you have to do each time you feel panicky. And it only works if the fear is irrational. Not all of your anxiety will be irrational."

"So, it does work then?" Nicole asked.

"Yes, if you can do it. I've only had one patient who managed to do it."

"So, if I call a panic attack on by thinking about something that makes me panic, the panicky feeling will go?" Nicole asked.

Miss Hastings nodded. "As long as you're panicking about something irrational. Do you feel brave enough to try it?"

"No. Even the thought of a panic attack terrifies me. I think I'll take the slow route."

They talked for another thirty minutes, but Nicole was not paying attention. Brad had been right. There was a way to beat panic attacks other than by taking tablets, but was she strong enough to do it?

Sheryl, Linda and Angela arrived as Nicole was showing Miss Hastings out. They were carrying suitcases.

"Goodbye, Miss Hastings," Nicole said.

"Goodbye, Nicole," Miss Hastings said. "I'll pop and see you in a couple of weeks. I'll phone first."

When her friends were in the house, Nicole closed the door. Now that she knew there was a way to beat panic attacks, she felt more optimistic about the future. If Brad's father could do it, there should be no reason why she could not do it.

"We've brought a few things," Sheryl said. "A change of knickers and that. Where's Brad?"

"He's sitting in the garden," Nicole said.

"Linda walked upstairs. "Come on. I want to show you my new underwear."

Chapter Eighteen

Brad and Nicole spent the week travelling around the Midlands with Sheryl, Linda, Angela and their three boyfriends, Mat, Mat and Mat. They called them Big Mat, Little Mat and Medium Mat. They were three decent lads, although Brad did not expect to see them again. Sheryl, Linda and Angela changed their boyfriends as often as they changed their shoes. It was a busy week, and Brad enjoyed himself. They went to Stratford-upon-Avon and Iron Bridge and spent the evenings in clubs and pubs.

Nicole's parents phoned to say they would be returning home on Saturday, so they brought the party forward to Friday and then cancelled it because of the short notice; only a few of their friends could make it.

At nine-thirty on Friday morning, Brad walked into the kitchen and sat down at the table. Nicole was cooking breakfast. Sheryl, Linda and Angela had gone home. "It's been one hell of a week," he said.

She turned around and smiled. "It has. I've really enjoyed myself."

"Do you want to hold hands?" he asked.

"Not while I'm cooking." They had been holding hands all week, but that was all she could do. She had been hoping that she would be able to hug him by now.

"Do you think we will ever have sex?" he asked.

"I hope so, eventually. The problem is, if I so much as think about kissing you or hugging you, I begin to panic. I can't even think about sex."

It was getting him down. He was living with a beautiful woman, and all he could do was hold her hand. "Don't worry. In a few weeks, I'll be fucking the living daylights out of you."

"I hope so. Do you want a coffee?"

"Yes. So, you do want to have sex with me?"

"Yes. I want us to be normal. I would like us to be boyfriend and girlfriend again. I don't want you to go rushing off to see Tina."

He had been to see Tina twice during the week. She had screamed once the first time and three times the second time. "I also want us to be normal. I spend my days with a beautiful woman I can't touch. It's too much for any man."

She sighed. "I know how you feel. I'm just as frustrated." She poured the boiling water into the cups. "I want to kill the bastards who raped me more than ever. Can we go after them tonight? I think it'll help me if I kill them."

"Yes. I also want to kill the bastards. Although the men I'm after might not be the men who raped you, and I'll be doing the killing."

“I think they are the same gang.” She put the cups on the table and stared at him. He might not understand, but she had to tell him. “If they are the men who raped me, I want to kill them. I need to kill them.”

He sipped his coffee. She seemed serious. “Are you sure? Killing someone is a messy business. If you shoot them, there will be blood everywhere.”

“I don’t care. I have to kill the men who raped me. I’ve never needed to do anything so much in my life.

He was not sure that it was a good idea, although he understood how she felt. He also needed to kill the men who had killed his mother. “I still can’t believe that my mother’s dead.”

“I can’t either. When is her funeral?”

“It was yesterday.”

She stared at him in disbelief. “Why didn’t you go?”

“I couldn’t. I wanted to.” He spread his hands. “I just couldn’t. I really loved my mother. I think she would understand.”

“I’m sure she would. I also hate funerals.”

They began to eat the meal.

She glanced at him. There was now a strong bond between them. It was very powerful. He needed a haircut and a shave. Could it be love? What was she thinking? Of course, it was love. She had never stopped loving him. “Do you love me?”

“Yes.”

She sighed. “Life’s such a bastard.”

“Tell me about it.”

At eight o’clock in the evening, they drove to Handsworth and parked a short distance from The Old Mill public house. He began to feel apprehensive, but as long as he wore his disguise, no one would recognise him. He lit a cigarette and then realised that he had not offered Nicole one. He held the packet out towards her. “I’m sorry. I wasn’t thinking.”

“No thanks. Are you wearing a bulletproof vest?”

“Yes. I will need to wear it every day as part of my job.”

“I won’t be wearing one,” she said. “It looks wrong even under my coat.”

They walked up to the public house and tried to act as if they were just going for a drink.

“We could sit outside the pub?” she said. “There’s a vacant table.”

“A good idea. We can then see who comes and goes.”

She sat down and put her handbag, containing her gun, onto the table in front of her. There were dozens of West Indians sitting outside the pub, but unless she heard them speak, she would not recognise the men who had raped her. She took the listening device out of her bag, put the earpiece into her ear and pointed it at likely suspects. She could hear everything they said as if they were sitting at her table.

As he walked into the bar to get the drinks, he saw the thug with the tattoo behind the ear. He was about thirty, tall and had a shaved head. Brad felt like shooting him there and then. By the time he had bought the drinks and walked outside, the thug had disappeared. He put the drinks on the table and sat down. "Can I have that pen, Nicole?" he asked. "I've just seen one of the bastards who killed my mother."

She suddenly felt nervous. This time, it was a rational fear, although it felt just as frightening. She gave him the pen and the earpiece. "Where is he?"

"He's in the pub." He put the earpiece in his ear and stood up. The thug with the tattoo behind his ear walked out of the bar with a drink in his hand, followed by another West Indian man. Brad sat back down. The two black men walked a short distance and leaned against a wall. They were about fifty feet away from Brad and Nicole. Brad pointed the pen at them and listened. He could hear them clearly.

"Are you sure, Sam?" the man with the tattoo said. Sam was about twenty-five, very tall, and also had a shaved head.

"Fucking right I am," Sam said. "I walked past her and had a close look. She's got the mole on the lip."

"Fucking hell," the man with the tattoo said. "Go and get Toss, George and Vic. Tell them to take a look."

Sam walked into the bar.

Brad suddenly realised that they were talking about Nicole. He glanced at her. She had a small mole just above her top lip. "What were the names of the men who raped you?"

"George, Sam, John, Vic and Toss. "Why?"

"See that tall black man with a shaven head in the blue shirt leaning against the wall," he said. "The one I'm pointing the pen at."

She glanced at him. "Yes."

"I think he's one of the men who raped you. I think his name's John. He's the one who killed my mother. The men walking out of the pub now are Toss, George, Vic and Sam. The very tall one in the white trainers is Sam."

She looked at them without making it obvious. Her heart was thumping wildly in her chest. These were the men who had raped her. They were the animals who used her as a blow-up doll and who were probably going to kill her when they had finished with her.

Brad aimed the pen at the group of men.

"What the fuck's going on, John?" a man with dreadlocks asked the man with the tattoo behind his ear.

"That man with the tattoo is named John," Brad said.

"She's sitting at that table with the bloke with long hair," John said.

"Are you sure?" the man with dreadlocks asked.

"Positive," John said.

"Give us a fag, Vic," the man with the dreadlocks said.

Vic was about thirty-five, short, muscular and had a beard. He gave the man with the dreadlocks a cigarette.

"The man with the beard is Vic," Brad said.

"What are you going to do?" Vic asked the man with the dreadlocks.

"Just stay here with John," the man with the dreadlocks said. "Me, Sam and Toss will have a shifty."

The three men walked towards them.

"I think the man with the dreadlocks is George," Brad said. "The men with him are Sam and Toss. Sam is the very tall one. The other man is Toss." Toss was about forty-five, muscular and ugly.

She glanced at them. They looked like the vicious animals she knew them to be. "What shall we do?"

"Sit tight," Brad said. "They've recognised you and want to make sure that it is you." He put his hand under his coat and placed it on the butt of his holstered gun. "They won't do anything in front of all these people."

She had a good look at the three men as they walked past her table. She wanted to make sure that she would never forget their faces. They stopped a few feet away. She opened her handbag and placed her hand on her gun. They would not be hurting her again. If they tried anything, she would kill them.

Brad glanced at the men, looking for the crooked finger. He could not see their hands. He felt nervous. It would look better if they talked. "It was a good party, wasn't it?"

"Yes," Nicole said. "I enjoyed it."

The three men had their backs to them and were obviously listening. George was about forty, tall, very muscular and had a huge chest.

"I don't like Steve," Brad said. "He's a big-headed bastard. Thinks he's God's fucking gift."

The three men began to walk back to John and Vic.

Brad noticed that Sam had a crooked little finger. He now knew who had killed his mother.

Nicole leaned back in her seat. She felt drained. It had been an ordeal, but it had been worth it. She now knew what the men who had raped her looked like. All she had to do now was kill them.

Brad finished his drink and took out his cigarettes. "Fucking hell. That was fucking close. We now know that the men who raped you are the same men who have been after me and who killed my mother. We can now plan what to do." He aimed the pen at the men."

"I feel like shooting them now," she said.

All five men were now leaning on the wall, looking towards them.

"What do you think, George?" John asked. "Is it her?"

"Yes," George, the man with the dreadlocks, said. "It's her all right, but what the fuck is she doing here?"

"The one with the dreadlocks is George," Brad said.

"What are they saying?" she asked.

"I'm trying to listen," Brad said.

"It could be a coincidence," Sam said.

"Like fuck it is," George said. "She came looking for us. Sam, get the knives and my piece from behind the bar. I'll teach her to come looking for me."

Sam walked into the bar.

"What are they saying?" Nicole asked.

"I think they are going to try to kidnap us," Brad said. "Sam, the man who has just gone into the bar, is going to get knives and a gun. We have to get away." Brad glanced about. "Pick up the glasses and walk towards the door behind us that leads to the lounge. Act as if you're going to get us another drink. When you're out of their sight, run back to the car and start the engine. I'll give you a two-minute start."

She slipped her handbag over her shoulder, picked up their empty glasses, and, without looking at the men who had raped her, walked towards the door to the lounge. There was a wall on the public house that jutted out. As soon as she was behind the wall and out of sight of the gang, she put the glasses down and walked around the side of the pub. When she was sure that no one was looking at her, she began to run towards her car.

Brad sat smoking with the pen aimed at the men.

"Are we going to fuck her again?" Vic asked.

"We might as well," George said. "This time, you can damage the merchandise. Then we'll kill the little bitch."

"Can I cut up her tits?" Vic asked.

"Not until I've fucked her," George said. "You can then cut her tits off and stick them up her arse for all I care, and you can take photos of her."

The men laughed.

Sam walked out of the bar, carrying a small bag.

Brad stood up and walked slowly towards the door of the lounge. The men began to walk towards him. As soon as Brad was out of sight of the men, he ran around the side of the pub and down the road. He glanced back. No one was following him.

Nicole had turned the car around and was waiting with the engine running. As soon as Brad climbed in, she drove off.

"Are you all right?" she asked.

"Yes." He was looking out of the back window for a sign of the men or of a car following them. When they were on College Road, heading towards Sutton Goldfield, he began to relax. "You can slow down now. We don't want to be done for speeding."

"Could you light me a cigarette?" she asked. "I've never done anything like that before. It was terrifying." The panic she had felt began to subside. "They're the nastiest men I've ever seen."

He lit two cigarettes and handed one to her. "You were fantastic. Them bastards are enough to terrify anyone. At least we now know what we're up against, and we know what they look like."

She inhaled deeply. "I can't wait to kill them."

He glanced at her. "Do you really think you can kill them?"

"Yes. I need to kill them. When are we going back?"

"I don't know. We should let things calm down first."

"I think we should go back tomorrow," she said. "I could put on a disguise, and you could shave your head. We could kill them before they knew what was happening."

"Hang on a bit," he said. "It won't be that easy, and we can't take on all five in one go. They're used to violence and could be armed, and they'll probably be experts with a gun. We'll have to take them two at a time. Three at the most."

She was eager to go back and kill at least one of them. "We can still go tomorrow."

"I suppose so."

He sat thinking. The thugs would not realise that they had made a run for it, although they would now be on the lookout for them. It could be very dangerous, and if he had any sense, he would never go back, but he had never had any sense. If they went back, he would try to kill Sam and John, the two men who had killed his mother. If he did, there would be no need to go after the others, and as much as Nicole claimed to want to kill them, she would not be able to. Very few women were capable of killing.

Chapter Nineteen

Brad and Nicole got drunk that night. Because of the tablets she was taking, Nicole only needed to drink a small amount to get inebriated. Brad had drunk at least eight cans of lager. At twelve o'clock, they walked hand in hand upstairs. She had found the gang who had raped her, and she was on a high.

"What did they say when you were listening to them?" she asked. "Did they say that they were going to kill me?"

"Yes." He decided not to tell her that they had intended to cut off her breasts. "I'm slightly drunk."

"I know." She stopped at her door. It would be nice to be able to hold Brad without feeling panicky. She kissed him on the lips and opened her door. "Aren't you supposed to turn into a prince or something?"

Her blouse was open, and he could see most of her right breast. "If you kissed me when I was on the motorway, I'd turn into a lay-by."

She did not know what he meant, but could not be bothered to ask.

"Do you realise that you kissed me on the lips?" he said.

"Oh yes. I did it without thinking."

"Could you have sex with me without thinking?" he asked.

"I wish I could. Goodnight."

"Goodnight." He opened his bedroom door and hit his shoulder on the doorframe. He was more than slightly drunk. He lay on the bed without getting undressed. The room was spinning around. It spun even faster when he closed his eyes. The trick was to try to follow the room with your eyes as it spun. He began to feel sick.

*

It took four cups of black coffee in the morning before Brad could focus his eyes. He was slumped in a chair in the kitchen. He looked up. Nicole was smiling at him. "It's not a laughing matter. I feel like death."

"You look like it, and get a shave. No. It will help to disguise you. Keep the beard, and I'll shave your head."

"How is it you haven't got a headache?" he asked. "You were drunk last night."

"I know, but I wasn't as drunk as you. Have you had a shower?"

He nodded. He felt green and had a thumping headache.

"Then go for a swim," she said. "I've already had a swim. It'll help clear your head."

"I think you're right." He slowly stood up and walked to the pool room. It was the last time. Definitely the last time. He was never going to get drunk again. Nothing was worth this amount of suffering.

She took her coffee into the pool room and sat and watched him swim slowly up and down on his back. She felt that she had almost recovered. She no longer had nightmares; her depression had gone, and she was looking forward to having a relationship with Brad. It was the panic attacks that were getting her down. She felt panicky when she was on her own, especially outside. She could also feel panicky at any time of the day or night for no reason at all, and if she tried to get near to Brad or touch him, her anxiety hit the roof. Brad's father must be very brave to have called on a panic attack.

She sipped her coffee. The fear she felt when she had a panic attack was irrational. When she saw the men who had raped her, she felt frightened, but she had not panicked. If she had panicked, it would have been a normal reaction. What was totally irrational and illogical was her fear of being touched by Brad. She trusted him and knew that he would never harm her. She would be as frightened of walking down to the shops on her own as she would be if she were being attacked by a tiger. It did not make sense. If only she could get rid of the feeling of anxiety that was with her for most of the time and conquer the panic attacks. She sighed. It was spoiling her life. If she were brave, she would call the panic on when she felt panicky, but she was not brave. Nothing in life frightened her as much as a panic attack.

The swim was very enjoyable, and he now felt ready for breakfast. "Do you still want to go after them?"

"Yes. Do you?"

"Yes. I want them bastards dead." He was thinking in particular about Sam and John.

"Touché," she said. "I was thinking. If you're going to work for my father … You are, aren't you?"

"Yes."

"Then you can't shave your head. You'll have to cut your hair short and wear a bald wig."

She was right. He was looking forward to working as a rep and did not want to upset her father. "Have you got a wig?"

"Yes. I've got several wigs. I'm going to wear a short blonde wig and heavy eye makeup. They won't recognise us. How are we going to kill them?"

"I've been thinking about that." He climbed out of the pool and dried himself. "We need to find out what vehicles they drive and follow them. I've been reading the literature that your father gave me. He sells bugs of all sorts. There are gadgets that can be put on a person or a car so that they can be followed. It's done by satellite. If we can borrow one, we can find out where they go and where they park their cars. Once we know where they hang out, we can lie in wait for them. Will your dad help us?"

"Yes. You can tell him that you want to test it on my car. Do you want breakfast?"

"Yes, but not a fry-up. Two boiled eggs and toast will do."

They were watching a film when her parents returned home. They looked tanned and happy.

"Did you have a good holiday?" Nicole asked.

"Yes," her mother said. "Is everything all right?"

"Yes," Nicole said. "Sheryl, Linda and Angela have been staying here. We've had a great week."

"I'm glad to hear that," her father said. "I need a drink. I'm parched." He walked into the kitchen.

"I'm going to have a bath and get changed," Nicole's mother said. "I'm worn out. I hate flying." She walked out of the lounge and upstairs.

"What would they say if they knew that we were thinking of killing five men?" Brad asked.

"I don't think they would believe us. I can't believe what we are going to do. I was always a coward when it came to violence. I never had a fight at school. My mother would be shocked, although I think my dad would understand."

Nicole's father walked into the room and sat down. "Are you ready to start work on Monday, Brad?"

"Yes. I can't wait. How long will I be training?"

"It all depends." Nicole's father took a long drink of lager. "You'll be working with Ben's son, David. He's got a business degree. Ben's my partner. You'll get on with them. They're very easygoing. They do most of the selling. I work mostly with admin. I chase orders and deal with the technicians who install the security systems. We have six installers, a couple of trainees and three office staff. Pat also works in the office. Business is good, and we now need another girl to help in the office and another technician. Ben's the expert. He even knows how some of the gadgets work."

"I'm dead keen," Brad said. "Will I have to travel?"

"Yes, eventually. Ben was in Israel a month ago. He's been to America and Russia. We do good business in Russia."

Brad was surprised. "Will I have to go abroad?"

"Not for a few years. I think they want you to deal with the home market. It'll mean some travelling, and if it's further than three hundred miles, you will fly."

At eight o'clock, they left her parents watching a video and drove to Handsworth.

She began to feel a ripple of nervous excitement flowing through her body. "Where are we going?"

"To The Old Mill. All we have to do is see what vehicles they drive and get the registration numbers."

"Just make sure we sit by a door or outside," she said. "I don't want us to get trapped."

"We can sit outside," he said.

They drove past The Old Mill public house. There were dozens of people sitting on the benches outside. He pulled into a side road and stopped the car. They tried on their disguises. He settled for a small beard and glasses. He had been wearing a long-haired wig without glasses before, so there was no way he would be recognised. "How do I look?" he asked.

"Very different. What does this wig look like?"

"All right."

He sat and watched her put on her makeup. She put on brown lipstick, blusher, and blue eyeshadow. It changed her appearance completely. "They won't recognise you like that. Just cover the mole up. They commented on your mole."

"It's a beauty spot," she said as she covered the mole with concealer. She put on a pair of glasses, pulled down the sun visor and looked in the vanity mirror. "That'll do."

They were wearing different clothes, and he felt confident that the thugs would not recognise them. They walked to the pub and leaned against a wall. There was no sign of the gang. It was a rough area, and there were more Asians and blacks than whites. The roads were dirty, and the houses were run-down. Brad was used to a working-class neighbourhood, but he felt nervous in Handsworth. The ambience was decidedly unfriendly.

"Wait here, and I'll get the drinks," he said. He left her standing by a low wall and walked into the public house. It was getting dark, and all they had to do was sit in the shadows and wait for the thugs to turn up. They were bound to have a vehicle of some sort.

Nicole lit a cigarette. She was standing in the shadows next to a tall brick pillar with an old-fashioned light at the top. It was an ideal spot to stand. She then saw John. He was sitting at a table with Sam. Sam stood up and walked into the public house. She did not know what to do. She had no way of warning Brad.

A few minutes later, Sam came out of the public house and began talking to John. They looked serious. Something had happened. Surely, he had not recognised Brad, but what if he had? The two men walked into the public house. She followed them.

*

Brad picked up the two drinks and walked towards the door. It was crowded in the large lounge, and he could not see any of the gang. When he walked down a hallway, past the toilets, someone grabbed him, pushed him against the wall and pressed the point of a knife against his throat. It was Sam. John was looking over Sam's shoulder.

"Are you sure it's him?" John asked. "He looks different to me."

"Yes," Sam said. "It's him all right. I recognised his voice at the bar. He also has a skull ring, the same as mine. Where's that bitch you were with last night?"

Brad had two drinks in his hand and could not move. "I wasn't here last night." He tried to disguise his voice.

Nicole walked into the passage and froze. Sam had a knife and had Brad pinned against the wall. The knife was pressed against Brad's neck. People were walking along the hall, but no one was prepared to get involved. She then remembered her gun. She took the gun out of her bag and walked towards them. Her hands were shaking, so she would have to get very close, or she would miss.

"You were fucking here," Sam said. "What the fuck are you up to? You had long hair last night. And you didn't have a beard." He pulled the false beard off Brad's face.

Brad had no choice but to admit that he had been at the public house. "I was here. I just didn't want anyone to know." He had to think of an excuse as to why he was wearing a disguise. "This girl I know is looking for her ex-husband."

"Where is she?" John asked.

"In the toilet," Brad said. "Her ex-husband's a big bloke, and I didn't want him to recognise me."

Nicole lifted up the gun in both hands and placed it a foot away from Sam's head. Her hands were shaking uncontrollably. As Sam turned around, she pulled the trigger.

There was a loud bang. Brad dropped the two glasses he was carrying and was covered in what felt like warm sick. Sam fell to the floor. For a split second, Brad did not know what had happened. He then saw Nicole with her gun in her hand. She had shot Sam in the head, and what he thought was warm sick on his face was Sam's blood and brains.

John recovered first, and he punched Nicole in the face. Nicole was knocked across the hall and fell to the floor. "You fucking bitch," John screamed.

Brad pulled his gun out of his shoulder holster at the same time that John pulled out a knife. Nicole was lying motionless on the floor. She looked dead. John took a step towards Nicole with the knife. Brad shot him in the back as he made to stab Nicole in the stomach.

John stood up, turned around and looked at Brad. "You bastard," he screamed. As John came at him with the knife in the air, Brad shot him in the face, and he fell over backwards. John, minus part of his face, lay twitching on the floor on top of Nicole. Brad had aimed at his chest and was surprised at how much kick there was on the gun. Brad glanced about. He could not see anyone. The place looked deserted.

Brad put his gun into his holster, picked up Nicole's gun and dragged the dead body of John off Nicole. He was huge and weighed a ton. He helped Nicole to stand up. She moaned and looked concussed but managed to support her own weight. "Are you all right?" he asked.

She felt confused, and everything looked hazy. It was as if she were standing in a smoke-filled room. "I don't feel very well. I think I fainted."

"We've got to leave," he said. He took her arm and led her out of the public house. There was no one sitting at the outside tables. Dozens of people were staring at them from across the road and from behind walls and doorways. "Can you run?"

"I'll try." She could not remember where she was or what was happening. It was very strange. She must be drunk. Brad was leading her by the arm. He seemed upset about something. "Where are we going?"

"We must hurry." Nicole managed to run with his help, and they ran down the side road towards the car. "Where are the car keys?"

"In my handbag."

When they reached the car, he took the keys out of her handbag, opened the driver's door and then the back door. "Get in the back." He pushed her into the back of the car and slammed the door. A dozen people were watching them from a distance. He climbed into the car and drove down the road.

"Don't be so rough," she said. She sat up. Her face hurt. She rubbed her face with her hand, and her memory switched back on in a flash. They had been at The Old Mill public house. They were now driving along the road. Brad was driving. She looked behind. "There's no one following us."

"Are you all right?" She sounded as if she had recovered.

"Yes. What happened? Did I kill him? I can remember shooting Sam. I think John hit me."

"John did hit you. You killed Sam." Brad turned right and then left and headed for Birchfield. "You shot Sam, and I shot John. They're both dead." He wiped his face with the back of his hand. "Fuck it. I'm covered in blood and brains."

She then realised that she was soaking wet. "I am as well." She clicked on her seat belt. He was driving fast. "Be careful. We don't want to crash."

He slowed down and glanced at her through the rear-view mirror. She looked wide-eyed and frightened. "I thought I was going to be stabbed. You saved my life. What made you come into the pub?"

"I saw Sam and John go after you. What happened when I was knocked down?"

"John went to stab you. I shot him in the back. When he turned around, I shot him in the face. I was aiming at his chest."

"It's a wonder I didn't miss," she said. "My hands were shaking. They still are."

"What are we going to do about all this blood?" he asked. "I'm covered in it."

"I don't know," she said. "We can't let my parents see us like this." She looked at her watch. It was just after eleven. She took her mobile phone out of her bag and phoned home.

"Hello?" her mother said.

"It's Nicole. We're having a good time. We might be late, so don't wait up."

"Your father's already gone to bed. I'm glad you phoned. I could do with a good night's sleep. I'll see you at breakfast."

"Yes," Nicole said. "Bye."

He parked the car where they could see Nicole's house and switched off the lights and the engine. The lounge and the hall lights were on. "We need to be prepared for what might happen."

She took out her cigarettes, handed him one and took one herself. "What do you mean?"

He lit their cigarettes. "Someone might have taken down the registration of your car. We could have the police knocking on your front door. Worse still, we could have George and his mates knocking on your door."

She began to worry. "What can we do?" She was beginning to respect Brad's clinical mind. He did not have any qualifications, but he had a high level of intelligence and common sense.

"If the police come calling, they're bound to find evidence of some sort," he said. "There's blood all over us and the car."

"We could burn the car," she suggested.

He drew on his cigarette. "We could. It would be the only way to get rid of the evidence. We could then claim that the car had been stolen."

"We could put our clothes into the car and burn them as well," she said.

"A good idea, but first, we need to get our story sorted out. We can tell the police, if they ask, that we went for a drink in Birmingham, to The George, and when we came out of the pub, we found that the car was missing. We then took a taxi home. We need to get a move on."

The lounge and then the hall light in her house went out.

"My mother's gone to bed. We can go in now."

They left the car where it was, crept into the house with their shoes in their hands and walked into the kitchen. "Where do you keep the black plastic bags?"

She took two plastic bags out of the cupboard. "Are these for our clothes?"

"Yes, and our shoes." He began to get undressed. "We need to put everything in the bags."

They stripped off down to their underwear, put their clothes into the plastic bags, and tiptoed upstairs to Nicole's bedroom. He was following Nicole. She had an unbelievable backside. He placed the black bag over his erection.

For some reason, she felt happy, really happy. She could not stop smiling. It felt as if they were playing a game. "I'll get a shower first," she whispered. "Turn around."

He turned around. He could see her in the dressing table mirror. He watched her take off her bra and pants and put them in one of the plastic bags. She had a beautiful figure. "I can see you in the mirror," he said.

She turned to look. He was grinning at her. "A gentleman wouldn't have looked," she said as she hurried into the en-suite bathroom.

"I'm not a gentleman, as well you know." He fetched a change of clothes from his room and stood thinking. It was not the police that he was worried about. It was George and his three mates. They must know who Nicole is and where she used to live, and it would not take an Einstein to find out where she is living now. If they were going to come looking for her, it would be within the next few days. They would have to be extremely careful.

She had a shower, slipped on her dressing gown and walked into the bedroom. He looked to be deep in thought. "It's all yours."

"You took your time," he said. He showered and changed in five minutes. Twenty minutes later, they were driving away from her house with the two plastic bags containing their clothes and a can full of petrol in the boot of the car. They were sitting on black bags so as not to get their clean clothes contaminated.

"I don't want you to stay at your house when I'm not with you," he said.

"Do you think George will come after us?" she asked.

"Yes. I could drop you off at one of your friends' houses on my way to work and pick you up on the way home."

"I have no intention of staying on my own," she said. "Not after what's happened. I'll be spending most of my time at the university. I should be able to catch up on my studies."

"If they do come, they'll be armed," he said. "They know we have guns, although they might not realise that it was us. I hope to God they don't. We were wearing disguises, and the two dead men will not be able to tell their mates that it was us. Did they speak on the phone when I was in the pub?"

"No."

"Good." The more he thought about it, the more convinced he became that George and his mates would not be coming after them. "Only Sam and John knew that we killed them. No one else knew. All that George will know is that it was a man and a woman."

"When are we going after them?" she asked.

He suspected that she was now too frightened to go after them. It was understandable. It had been a harrowing experience. He had killed the two men who had killed his mother, and so it suited him to never set foot in Handsworth again. "We don't have to go after them. We can forget about them now. You'll be moving house soon, and we can enjoy our life."

She felt disappointed. "We have to go back. I have to kill them."

He glanced at her. She was serious. "We killed two of them."

"I want them all dead." She could sense that he did not want to go after them. "I'll go on my own if I have to."

"If that's how you feel, then we'll both go after them," he said.

"Even though we have killed the men who killed your mother, it would have been George who would have given the order to beat up your family," she said.

She was right. They all deserved to die. It would be nerve-racking to live the rest of their lives worrying that George and other gang members would come after them. "We'll give it a few weeks to calm down, find a new disguise, get a new car, and go after them."

They parked the car in a side street, covered it inside and out with petrol, and set it alight. It burned like a huge bonfire. They ran down the road and headed for the centre of Birmingham. They wanted to be far away from the burning car when they hailed a taxi.

It was three o'clock when they returned to Nicole's house. He was exhausted. He followed her upstairs to their rooms. "If the police do turn up, just remember to stick to our story. Don't let them trick you."

"Don't worry. I know exactly what to say." She kissed him on the lips. "Goodnight. I'll see you tomorrow."

"Yes. Goodnight."

He undressed and crawled into bed. If the police came sniffing around, there was no evidence to link them to the deaths of the two blacks, and it was very unlikely that George would come after them. He smiled. It had been a job well done. The killers of his mum were dead.

Chapter Twenty

Brad and Nicole lived on their nerves each day. She was sure they were becoming paranoid, but when, after several weeks, they had not had a visit from the police or from George and his gang, they began to relax and enjoy life. Brad lost himself in work, and she lost herself in her studies, playing the violin and trying to overcome her revulsion of men. It was now six weeks since they had killed Sam and John, but all she could do was hold Brad's hand and kiss him on the cheek and sometimes on the lips. She desperately wanted them to have a proper relationship. She suspected that he still visited Tina once or twice a week, and it annoyed her that she could not satisfy him. She loved Brad, and she was jealous of Tina.

She was standing in the doorway of the bathroom, watching him shave. It was five-thirty in the evening. "You don't have to come," she said. "I know you don't like classical music."

"I wouldn't miss it for the world," he said as he shaved his neck. "I've flown back from Scotland to see you play. I'm very proud of you playing in the Birmingham Philharmonic Orchestra. There's nothing as good as a razor blade. If I use an electric shaver, it looks as if I haven't shaved." He kissed her on the cheek.

She wiped her cheek. "That was wet. We have to leave now. Mum and Dad have already gone on ahead. Are we taking your BMW?"

"Yes. I wish the car was mine." He put on his bulletproof vest, his shirt, and a tie.

"You don't have to wear your bulletproof vest tonight," she said.

"I wear it every day. It could save my life one day, and it's also a sales gimmick. I sell dozens of vests." He put on his suit jacket. "How do I look?"

"Very handsome."

They walked down the stairs.

"You haven't said how I look?" she said.

She was wearing a black evening dress. "You look beautiful. You're the most beautiful woman I've ever seen."

"Don't go overboard," she said.

"I wouldn't say it if I didn't mean it. It's what I thought when I first saw you standing at that bus stop."

She looked at him. He seemed serious. "Do you really mean that?"

"Yes, I do." And he did.

They climbed into the works BMW, and he drove them to Birmingham Symphony Hall. "Are you nervous?" he asked.

"Yes. It's my big break." It was her three-minute solo that she was worried about. She had, as a junior, played a solo part dozens of times, but this time it was different. Many of the music elite would be there. "I'm usually all right once I get started."

"You'll do just fine," he said. "I don't know how anyone can get a tune out of a violin. All that comes out when I run the bow across the strings is a screech." She could also play the piano and the guitar. "Why did you take up the violin?"

"My grandmother was a symphony violinist in London. As a child, I used to play one of her old violins in my bedroom. On my sixth birthday, I played my first solo. My grandmother was amazed and claimed I was a prodigy, and I started to have lessons. I love music. When I play, I can forget everything. It's been good therapy for me."

"I also feel the same …" He had been about to say when I have sex. She was still funny about sex, and tonight was not the night to bring it up. "… when I listen to music. I only wish I could play something other than the triangle. Mind you, I was good at the triangle. When my music teacher heard me, she said I was a prodigy. I think I misheard what she said. What she probably said was that I was a sodding b."

She smiled. "I bet you were."

Brad sat in the huge symphony hall next to Nicole's parents, Ben and his wife Jill, and David and his pregnant wife, Jackie. Ben and Jill were both small, fat and friendly. David, who was handsome, was also easygoing. Jackie was the odd one out. She was pretty, moody, a snob and decidedly unfriendly. She was telling them about her horses. Brad was sitting between Nicole's father and Ben and was able to ignore her.

According to Nicole's father, it was a privilege to play in such a prestigious orchestra. The orchestra was warming up. He could see Nicole, who was talking to a woman.

*

Nicole felt like screaming. One of the strings on her violin had snapped. "How could it happen tonight of all nights?"

"Don't worry," Lucinda said. "It's fixed now, and it sounds perfect. It happened to Nigel Kennedy last week. He's here, by the way. We might meet him later on."

"Is he?" Nicole was amazed. Nigel was her hero. "You shouldn't have told me. He's sure to notice all my mistakes."

Lucinda smiled. "You make very few mistakes, even on a bad day. Just close your eyes and imagine you're playing just for me in my little room."

"I'll do my best."

*

Brad's stomach rumbled. It was very loud and sounded like a dying cat. A woman in front of him turned around and gave him a questioning look. "It's all right," Brad said. "My stomach's just warming up. It'll sound better later on." The woman did not smile, but Nicole's father did.

The music was not to Brad's taste. When the orchestra began to play, it sounded to him as if they were still warming up. Nicole should do well. She had been practising for weeks. He lost interest after Nicole's solo and catnapped. He was knackered.

*

Nicole took several deep breaths when it was over. She had not made any glaring mistakes. She was led to the front of the stage by the conductor and took a little bow.

"You were great," the conductor said.

"Thank you," she said.

It was always the same. The time flew by when she was playing. It only seemed as if she had been playing for ten minutes and not thirty-five minutes. She put her violin away in its case and tried to see Brad in the audience. She could not locate him. The symphony hall was packed.

"You did absolutely splendid, Nicole," Lucinda said. "I knew you would. Come on. I want you to meet several important people."

*

Brad joined the others in the bar for a drink. He could not understand what they saw in this kind of music. They seemed to get so emotional about it. It would not be so bad if it had a tune of some sort. A man with a scruffy hairstyle was talking to Nicole. It was best if Brad kept to the background. These were not his kind of people.

"Did you enjoy it, Brad?" Nicole's father asked.

"No," Brad said. "But don't tell Nicole. I'm very glad that she's doing well, but I've never been so bored."

"I'm very proud of her," Nicole's father said. "But I know what you mean. I'm not a fan of classical music. I only came to see Nicole."

*

Nicole was in a daze. Nigel Kennedy had complimented her on her solo and said that she was one of the top twenty violinists in England. She had also been asked to play in Manchester next week. She drank more than she should and was a little drunk when Brad drove her home. He looked very tired. "You look as if you need a holiday," she said.

"I could do with one. We could go somewhere warm. What about Greece?"

"I'd love to go to Greece. When?"

"Any time, but only for a long weekend. We can have a week just after Christmas. I've decided to do an A-level in business studies at the National Extension College. It'll give me something to do when you practise the violin. I'd like to eventually get a degree."

"I'm pleased." She sat for a while thinking. He did not seem very eager to go after the men who had raped her. "We could go to Greece this weekend, and when we get back, we could go after the men who raped me."

"Greece is a good idea," he said, but let's leave it until after Christmas before going after the men who raped you. By then, they'll have relaxed their guard."

"I want to go after them before Christmas," she said. "I want it over and done with."

"Okay." It did not look as if he had any choice. He had expected that, in time, she would lose interest in the men who had raped her and get on with her life. He had been wrong. Nicole was not an ordinary run-of-the-mill woman. She was very special in many ways. One was in the bust department. God, if only he could get his hands on her tits.

Chapter Twenty-One

Brad and Nicole flew to Greece on Friday evening. He had flown several times for his job, but would rather drive. He could not get his head around the physics of flight. It did not seem right that a hundred-ton aircraft could lift off the ground. Just before they took off, he had seen a news flash about a plane crash in America. All two hundred people on board had been killed. It had made him a nervous wreck. They landed in Greece without any problems. It was warm, even though it was almost ten o'clock in the evening. They caught a taxi to their hotel.

Nicole had booked a single room in the name of Mr and Mrs Shaw. She was determined to have sex with Brad, even if she had a dozen panic attacks. They had a couple of drinks in the bar of the hotel, which was seedier than the travel agent had led her to believe and walked up to their room on the first floor. The room was sparse, and the walls were in need of a coat of paint.

"I hope the bed linen and towels are clean," she said. "It's not the cleanest place I've been in."

"There's only one bed," he said. "I hope I'm not going to have to sleep in the bath."

"No. We'll be sleeping together."

"Why?" He was praying that she was going to have sex with him.

"I thought it might help me, but don't try anything. I want you to keep to your side of the bed."

He felt disappointed. "I thought I was going to have a bit."

"That's the intention, eventually. Just don't rush me. I don't know if it's going to work."

He was hoping it would work. He was sick of having to visit Tina. Paulette had told him that Tina was having sex with a dozen different men and was now sleeping with a woman. It was no longer a scream.

They undressed in the dim light coming in from the bathroom and climbed into bed. He had his shorts on, and she was wearing a nightie. He already had an erection.

She felt anxious but managed to keep her panic under control by assuring herself that she was not going to touch him and that nothing was going to happen. They lay about a foot apart. Why she should be afraid of Brad, she had no idea. She wanted to touch him and to have sex with him. It did not make sense.

"Are you all right?" he asked.

"Not really. I'm sick of being ill. Just don't try anything."

"I won't."

After what seemed like an eternity, she fell asleep.

*

They spent the day sightseeing and walking along the beach. It was as hot as a summer day in England. They held hands, and to anyone watching, they would appear to be a normal couple. They were anything but normal. What made things worse was that she now desired Brad. She had reduced her tablets, and her feelings had returned, and she wanted to have sex. Her powerful desire for sex was at war with her even more powerful fear of having a panic attack.

Nicole had never looked so beautiful and sexy, and if Brad had to spend another night lying next to her without being able to do anything, it would send him mad. Perhaps tonight would be different. Perhaps he would be able to grab her tits, and … He blew out his cheeks. He would have to try to think about something else.

She had three drinks that evening, and they undressed and lay down on the bed next to each other in the near darkness. She was even more nervous and almost had a panic attack. Not being able to have sex was beginning to get her down. What was the point of living if she could not have sex? She would not be able to get married or have children. She cried herself to sleep.

He lay awake after she had fallen asleep. He felt guilty. Sleeping together was not helping.

*

The next day, they had breakfast and went for a walk through the narrow streets of the town. Her crying the night before had upset him. She had suffered so much and was still suffering all because of those murdering bastards. He decided to tell her a joke. "A man had all his fingers chopped off, and he ran to the hospital. The doctor said, Why didn't you bring your fingers with you? The man said, I wanted to, but I couldn't pick them up."

She tried to smile but failed. She felt too depressed to smile. "I'm sorry I'm so miserable. I was determined to overcome my problem so that we could have sex. I even bought some condoms and sexy underwear. The problem is, as soon as I even think about sex, I start to panic. I then can't do anything. It's making me depressed."

He felt sorry for her and, despite her reluctance, he decided to try to help her. "Have you got your tablets?"

"Yes."

"Hold the bottle in your hand." He would have to put pressure on her; otherwise, she might never get better.

She took the bottle of tablets out of her bag. "What do you want me to do?"

"Get ready to take them."

"What are you going to do?" She was already beginning to feel anxious.

"Nothing. How many tablets would you need to take to stop a panic attack?"

"Just one. Why? If I take tablets every time I want to do something, within a month, I'll be on a hundred a day. I'm trying to reduce the number of tablets I'm taking."

"I don't want you to take them," he said. "They're just there so that you know that you can take them at any time and kill the panic attack."

"Are you expecting me to call it on?" she asked.

"Yes."

"I can't."

He squeezed her hand. "You can. You've got the tablets if it doesn't work. What have you got to lose? Having one extra panic attack won't make much difference in the long run, and if it doesn't work, you can forget about it."

"It's not as easy as that," she said. "Could you imagine how you would feel if you were tied down and someone with a chainsaw was about to cut off your legs? The panic I get, even though it's over nothing, is as bad as that. A panic attack is always as bad, for whatever reason, a person panics."

"I don't know what else I can do," he said. He had intended to put his arm around her waist to bring on a panic attack so that she could call it on, but he decided not to. She would have to do it on her own.

She felt like screaming. "I just can't do it. I'm not strong enough."

"I think you are. My dad did it."

"I'm not a brave person like your dad. She was on the brink of tears. She was also very angry with herself for being so weak. If his dad could do it, then she should be able to. Sod it. She was going to do it, and if it killed her, it killed her. She imagined Brad feeling her breasts and then climbing on top of her. She felt herself beginning to panic. "You bastard."

He stopped and let go of her hand. "I'm sorry. I didn't mean to upset you. I was only trying to help."

"I'm not shouting at you. I'm calling the panic on. Come on, you bastard. Come on. Come on."

Several people stopped and stared at them. He felt embarrassed.

"Come on, you bastard," she screamed. "You fucking bastard."

She stopped screaming and stared in front of her. Her eyes were wide open.

"What are you looking at?" he asked. "Are you all right?" He was worried that she had gone completely round the bend.

She turned and looked at him. She could not believe it. The panic had come at her as if it were a wild beast, but as soon as she mentally reached out to grab it, to kill it, it disappeared completely. She was shocked. "I don't believe it."

"What? What don't you believe?"

"It worked."

"What did?" The people who had been watching them began to walk away. One of them touched her temple. They obviously thought Nicole was mad.

"The panic. I called it on, and it disappeared."

"You did. It did." He did not know what to do. "Has it completely gone?"

"Yes. Completely. Hug me."

He was a little apprehensive. She might begin to panic again, and he was not very good with panicking women. He put his arms around her. He was hardly touching her. "What's happening?"

"Nothing."

He pulled her to him and gave her a real hug. "Is anything happening now?" He prayed that she would not panic. He was enjoying the feel of her large breasts pressed against his chest.

She searched her mind for the anxiety that was always lurking there. There was no trace of it. "No. I feel normal." For the first time since being raped, she felt like a human being with normal human feelings.

"Can I kiss you?" he asked. It might be his only chance of kissing her.

"Yes." He kissed her on the lips. She could feel his tongue in her mouth. There was no sign of the panic. She began to feel aroused. She had forgotten how nice it was to be kissed. She pulled away, grabbed his hand and ran down the road.

He began to worry. "Where are we going? Are you panicking?"

"No. I'm fine. I've never felt so good. We're going to the hotel. I want you to make love to me. Are you up to it?"

He could not believe it. "Are you serious?"

"Yes. I want you to fuck me before the panic comes back."

He tried to remember what his dad had said about calling the panic on. Perhaps it did not last very long the first time. "Is it coming back?" he asked as they ran into the hotel."

"No." There was no sign of the panic, but she was not sure how long it would last. It was as if she had taken a powerful drug.

They ran upstairs and into their bedroom. She threw off her dress and got a condom out of her bag. He was throwing off his clothes. "Hurry up."

"I'm going as fast as I can. Are you panicking?"

"No." She lay down on the bed and opened her legs. There was still no sign of the panic. She would know in a few seconds if it had worked.

He rolled on the condom. God, did she look sexy. Her pants were pulled tight over her pubic mound. He climbed onto the bed, pulled her pants to one side and pushed his throbbing penis into her. It was fantastic. He thrust into her, squeezed her breasts and climaxed. His body shuddered as the power of the climax tried to kill him. It almost succeeded. He collapsed on top of her. He had waited so long to have sex with her.

She lay with him on top of her and waited for the panic to come. Nothing happened. Her mind was calm and free of anxiety. She hugged him and wrapped her legs around him. There was still no sign of the panic.

"Do you want me to get off?" he asked.

"No. Stay there. As soon as you feel up to it, I want you to fuck me again and this time I want to climax."

"It could take a few minutes. I'm usually a once-a-day man."

"I just hope I don't suddenly panic again." She hugged him. It felt wonderful to hold him close. "I want to make the best of this moment." She began to kiss his neck and run her nails up and down his back. "Do you feel sexy yet?"

"Give me a chance. I've only just come." He began to squeeze her huge breasts. God, they were beautiful. "I've been dying to get my hands on these. How do you feel?"

"Good. I now feel aroused, and I need to be fucked like mad."

"Is there any sign of the panic?" he asked.

"No."

"The way you were shouting," he said. "I think you frightened it to death."

She smiled. "If I get my hands on it, I'll kill it." She pressed her hips against him. "Come on."

"Bleeding hell," he said. "One minute, you don't want it, and the next, you're crying out for it." He began to get an erection and checked that the condom was on. "Hold tight. We're about to try for the airspeed record." He began to thrust into her.

The pleasure she felt began to fill her mind and body. There was no sign of the panic. His naked body felt heavenly against her flesh. The pleasure was now washing over every nerve of her body. It was better than it had ever been. The pleasure became too large for her body, and it exploded and seemed to burst through her skin. "Ohhhhh," she cried out. "Ohhhhhh. Ohhhhhh. Ohhhhhhhh."

He squeezed her breasts and climaxed for a second time. It was every bit as wonderful, and the pleasure hit him over and over again. He lay in the afterglow of the climax and gently squeezed her left breast. They had done it at last. He was praying that they would be able to do it on a regular basis. "I think we broke the sound barrier."

"I think we did. I really needed that. I feel as if my tits have been put through a mangle. Did you enjoy it?"

"Yes." He kissed her on the lips. "It's difficult not being able to make love to the woman you love."

"It was difficult for me as well. Is that condom still on?"

"Yes. Shall I take it off?"

"Yes, but be quick."

He climbed off the bed, took off the condom, put on his shorts, and lay back down next to her. He put his arm around her and played with her nipples. "I can't get enough of these."

"They're all yours." It was the first time she had felt normal since being raped. There was no sign of the panic, and she felt that she could do what she wanted. She ran her hands over his body. "Let's stay in bed. I don't want to move."

"Suits me."

They had sex that evening and again in the morning and returned to England as a proper couple. She felt that he was now her boyfriend. There was still no sign of the panic. According to what Brad had said, it would return, but the real cure was not to be afraid of it. It was the fear of fear that gave the panic its power. If it did return, she would call it on and try to wring its bleeding neck.

They arrived home in the early hours, quietly let themselves in and went up to bed without waking up Nicole's parents. This time, they climbed into the same bed. He felt that everything would be perfect from now on. They were both knackered and fell asleep in each other's arms.

*

Someone was shouting. Brad opened his eyes. Where was he? What was going on? Nicole's father was standing in the middle of the bedroom.

"Come in here, Pat," Nicole's father shouted.

"I'm coming," Nicole's mother shouted from the landing. "What's the matter?"

Brad sat up in bed. He was in Nicole's bed with Nicole. Fuck it. "It was ... I ..." It would be pointless denying that they had slept together. There was going to be an unholy row.

Nicole's mother walked into the room and put her hands to her face. She looked shocked. "Oh, my God."

"I'm sorry," Brad said. "We ..."

Nicole sat up. "What's wrong?"

"There's nothing wrong," her father said. He smiled and shook his head. "Absolutely nothing wrong."

Brad was relieved. "So, you're not upset then?"

"No," Nicole's mother said. "We've been praying that this would happen."

"Did you do it?" Nicole's father asked.

Brad smiled. "Yes. I think you can say that we did it."

Her mother walked over to Nicole and kissed her on the cheek. "I'm so pleased."

"You always said that you would kill the man who deflowered me," Nicole said to her father.

He spread his hands. "This is different. Let's celebrate. I know. We'll go out for a meal. We'll phone Ben and Jill."

"What will we say if they ask why we are celebrating?" Nicole asked.

They laughed.

Chapter Twenty-Two

Brad finished his breakfast and walked into the lounge. It was almost time for him to go to work, but he had promised to give Nicole a lift into Birmingham. There was no sign of her. He walked into the hall. "Are you up there?"

"Yes," she shouted. "I'm having a bath." Her period had started, and she felt better after a bath.

"Have you got any fags," he shouted. If she was having a bath, she would be at least thirty minutes, and he might as well watch the news on the television.

"No. You smoked the last one last night."

"Fuck it," he said. He needed a fag.

"There's a packet in my car," she shouted. "I'm putting on a CD. I'll be about twenty minutes."

Music began to blare out. She always played the music loud when she had a bath. He opened the front door. It was tipping it down, and her car was parked on the other side of the drive. "Fuck it." He picked up her car keys and took Nicole's father's golfing umbrella out of the rack. It was only thirty metres to the car, but if he did not use the umbrella, he would get soaked. He opened the umbrella and ran to her car.

*

Nicole sank slowly into the hot water. She was now a different person. She still did not like being on her own, but she had completely gotten over her revulsion of men. She was now mentally able to separate the good men from the bad. Everything was happening. A week on Saturday, she would be playing her violin in London, and next week, they would be moving to a beautiful Victorian house in Dorridge, and most wonderful of all, Brad had asked her to get engaged. It would be years before they got married, but it showed that he really loved her. She was planning a lavish engagement party.

*

Brad opened the car door and felt something hit him on the back of the head. He clutched his head and dropped the umbrella. He was barely able to stand. Someone spun him around, and he fell into a sitting position with his back against the side of the car. A man was standing above him. It was Vic

"It's him," Vic said.

"Then kill the bastard," George, who was out of Brad's sight, said.

Vic lifted a handgun and pointed it at Brad's chest.

"No," Brad shouted.

Vic shot him twice in the chest, and Brad felt his body jerk. The pain was excruciating. It felt as if he had been kicked in the chest by a horse. He could barely breathe.

"You shouldn't have messed with us," Vic said.

George and Toss appeared from the left and walked towards the front door. "Come on," George said. "Let's get the bitch."

Brad watched the three men walk into the house. He had left the front door wide open. It could not be easier for them. He had been wearing his bulletproof vest, so he should have been all right, but the vest had not worked. It was only a thin vest and was not designed to stop high-calibre bullets. He had felt the bullets rip into his chest. Vic must have used a very powerful gun. He pushed his hand beneath his vest, and it came out covered in blood.

He could only just breathe and probably had only minutes to live. He had to try to help Nicole. Above the sound of the rain, he could hear her music. He took his gun out of his shoulder holster. The men had gone into the house, and the front door was now closed. He tried to think. In a few seconds, they would be killing Nicole. No. They would probably rape her first. He had to do something, but what? How could he warn her? It would be useless to shout. The noise of the rain plus the music would drown out his shouts.

He squinted through the rain that was running down his face. He could just see the top corner of Nicole's en-suite bathroom window. He lifted his gun and aimed. With the rain lashing down, it was very difficult. He pulled the trigger, and the window broke.

*

Nicole was shocked, and she dropped the soap. Someone had thrown a brick through the window, and bits of glass had flown everywhere. Who would ... She then noticed what looked like a bullet hole in the ceiling. Someone had shot a bullet through her window. Why would anyone do such a thing?

She climbed out of the bath. It did not make sense. Why would someone shoot the glass out of her window? She slipped on her dressing gown and looked into her bedroom. There was no one there. She took her gun out of her bag, ran to the open bedroom door and looked out. She could not see anybody, and because of the loud noise of the CD, she could not hear anything. Where was Brad? Could he have been outside and accidentally fired his Gun? It was very unlikely.

She tiptoed along the landing and walked into her parents' bedroom. She was now very scared, and her hands were shaking. She switched on the security monitor. A picture of the kitchen appeared. A man was walking across the kitchen towards the back door. It was Vic, and he had a gun in his hand. She switched to the camera in the hall. George, who also had a gun, was going into her father's study. She switched to the camera in the lounge. Toss was by the television. He also had a gun. She switched to the camera covering the drive and gasped. Brad was sitting, leaning against her car. There was blood on his shirt. He looked dead. No. His hand moved. He was not dead. He had his gun in his hand. He had shot the window in the bathroom to warn her.

What could she do? They had obviously shot Brad and left him for dead. She had to get Brad to hospital as soon as possible, but how could she? She would first have to get past three armed men. She flicked the monitor from camera to camera. Vic had gone out of the back door. George had disappeared (he had probably gone into the garage), and Toss was walking across the lounge. She switched to the drive. Brad was still sitting in the pouring rain next to her car. While flicking back and forth (she had to know where the men were at all times), she tried to think what to do. Her mind was filled with fear, and she was finding it difficult to sort out her thoughts.

*

Brad was angry with himself. He should have been more careful. Vic walked around the side of the house and walked towards him. Brad hid the gun under his arm.

"Aren't you dead yet?" Vic said. "A bullet in the head will sort you out. You shot my mate in the fucking head."

As Vic lifted his gun, Brad shot him in the stomach. Vic staggered back. Brad shot him twice more in the chest, and Vic fell to the ground.

*

Nicole had watched Brad shoot Vic and then try to stand. He was not dead, but was probably severely injured. They now had one less man to deal with. She switched from camera to camera. She had to do something, and running was not an option. She could never leave Brad.

*

Brad managed to stand. He was in severe pain and could only take short, painful breaths. The bullets must have missed the vital organs, and he might have enough time left to save Nicole. He walked over to Vic, who looked dead, and tried to bend down to pick up Vic's gun, but was unable to. The pain in his chest was too great.

*

Nicole was relieved to see Brad on his feet. She switched the monitor back to the camera in the lounge. George was walking across the lounge. She switched to the hall. Toss was already halfway up the stairs with his gun held out in front of him. If she opened the bedroom door, she would be able to see him through the balustrade. She was tempted to open the door and take a shot at him. It would not be wise, at least not with him looking towards the room she was in. He was bound to be good with a gun and would probably shoot her before she could shoot him. She stood with her hand on the side of the door, watching the monitor and waiting for him to look away.

*

Brad moved the gun away from Vic with his foot and pushed it behind a flowerpot. They could be raping Nicole, and so he had to hurry. The rain was pouring down, and he was soaked to the skin. He walked slowly towards the front door. The pain in his chest was excruciating.

*

She switched to the camera in the lounge. George was not there. She switched to the drive. Brad was walking towards the door. She switched to the hall. Toss was still there. He was looking down the stairs. She opened the door. She could see the head of Toss through the balustrades. Her hands were shaking. She aimed and fired, and his head disappeared. She closed the door and looked at the monitor. Toss was lying upside down on the stairs. He was not moving. George ran to Toss, examined him and then began to walk slowly up the stairs with his gun held out in front of him.

*

Brad reached the front door. It was locked. He searched in his pocket for his keys. By now, they could have raped and killed Nicole. He could just hear the loud music over the sound of the rain.

*

Nicole switched from camera to camera. Brad was next to the front door, and George was walking up the stairs, but the rest of the house was empty. She took several deep breaths. Her hands were still shaking. The loud music was beginning to get on her nerves. George pushed the spare bedroom door with his foot and then went in. He came out and did the same to the bathroom and then to her bedroom. He then walked towards her parents' door. She stood about three feet from the door, aimed her gun at the door at about waist height and watched the monitor. She could only see George's feet.

*

Brad took the keys out of his pocket. A pain shot through his chest each time he moved. He unlocked the door and pushed it open. The music was blaring away, and he could not see anyone. He looked behind to make sure that no one was creeping up on him and then stepped into the hall.

*

George stepped in front of her parents' bedroom door, and she fired two shots while looking at the monitor. George fell and began to crawl away on his hands and knees. His gun was not in his hand. She opened the door, stepped out and shot him in the back. He fell onto his side and looked at her.

The gunshots sounded close, and at first, Brad thought that someone was shooting at him. When he realised that they were shooting at someone else, he stepped forward and looked up the stairs. A man was lying on the stairs, and another man was lying on the landing. Nicole was pointing her gun at the man on the landing.

"Don't kill me," George said.

George's gun was behind her, and she was too far away from him for him to grab her. She aimed the gun at his chest. "You bastard. You raped me."

"Don't kill me," George pleaded. "I'm shot. Get me to a hospital."

She had an overwhelming desire to hurt him. "You're an animal."

Brad was watching her. At one time, he believed she was not capable of killing someone. How wrong he had been. She looked calm and totally in control.

"I'm going to kill you," she said. "I've waited a long time to do this. You picked the wrong woman when you raped me." She shot George in the chest. He jerked and lay still. His eyes were closed. She aimed at his head and fired. The bullet missed. She aimed again and fired. This time, the bullet hit his head. There was now a hole in his head, just behind the ear, and blood was spreading across the carpet.

"Are you all right?" Brad shouted.

"Yes." She ran down the stairs and checked that Toss was dead. He had a huge hole in the top of his head. She walked up to Brad. He was leaning against the wall. He was soaking wet and covered in blood. "My God. Have you been shot?"

He sat down heavily at the bottom of the stairs. "Yes. I can hardly breathe. Are you all right? Did they touch you?"

"No. I'm all right. I've got to get you to hospital, but first, I've got to stop the bleeding." He had been shot in the chest and would be bleeding internally. He could die within minutes.

"The pain is unbearable," he said.

"Why weren't you wearing your vest?" she asked. She was beginning to choke up. "You always wear your vest."

"I am wearing it, but the bullets have gone through it."

She helped him take off his coat and his shirt. She could see where the bullets had gone through the vest. "I've got to get the vest off." The loud music was driving her mad.

He lifted his arms so that she could take off the bulletproof vest. It felt as if his chest had caved in.

She wiped the blood off his chest with his shirt. There was only a small amount of blood and one bullet hole. She could see the bullet sticking out of his flesh. "There's only one bullet hole. I can see the bullet. It must have hit a rib."

He looked down. There were two huge bruises, but only one bullet hole. The vest must have stopped one bullet and partially stopped the other bullet. Perhaps he was not going to die. The bullet, which resembled a twisted piece of metal, was sticking out of his chest. "It hasn't gone in very far."

It did not look like a bullet. She touched it. The vest must have disfigured it. She slowly pulled it out of his chest and held it up in front of her. "What sort of bullet is this? It looks like a twisted cross."

He looked at the bullet. It did look odd. "I think ..." He then realised what it was. "It's not a bullet. It's my St Christopher. The bullet must have hit it."

There was very little blood coming out of the wound. "You haven't been shot then." She sat down on the stairs and began to cry. "I thought ... you ... were ..." She could not speak.

He put his arm around her shoulders. The relief he felt was overwhelming. He had been convinced that he was going to die. It had been a terrifying feeling. He leaned back against the wall and closed his eyes. The vest had saved his life. The vest had worked. It was as good as he had been claiming it was.

"Oh, fuck it," she screamed. "That music's driving me mad." She ran upstairs and switched it off. She walked slowly down the stairs and sat next to him. She felt drained.

"Are they all dead?" he asked.

"George and Toss are," she said. "Is Vic dead?"

He nodded. "We did it. We've killed all of them." He felt much better now that he knew that he was not going to die. "All the men who raped you are dead."

She sighed. "Yes. I was scared. I thought ... I'm glad you were wearing that vest."

"Not as glad as I am. What do we do now? How do we get rid of three dead bodies?"

She stood up. "The first thing I'm going to do is get the cigarettes and a drink." She returned with the cigarettes and two cans of lager, and for a while, they sat on the stairs, drinking and smoking.

"Did they come in a vehicle?" he asked.

"Yes. There's a Transit van parked a few metres down the road. "What are we going to do?"

"Put them in their van, drive them back to Handsworth, and set fire to the van. There will then be nothing to tie us in with them unless they told someone where they are going, which I doubt. Whatever happens, deny knowing anything."

"What about the blood?" she asked. "It's everywhere."

"The carpet is dark red, so it shouldn't be too difficult to mop it up," he said.

"Are you up to mopping?" she asked.

He stood up. The pain was just as bad. "No, but I'll do my best. I'd better phone your father. I'll tell him that I fell down the stairs."

After phoning Nicole's father, they parked the Transit van by the front door, and between them, they dragged and then lifted Vic into the back of the van. "I think I must have a couple of broken ribs," he said. "Do you have any painkilling tablets?"

"Yes. I'll get them. I also need another drink."

It took them three hours to get the men into the back of the van, mop up the blood and wipe the walls. They then showered, changed, and put their soiled clothes into a black plastic bag.

He looked at Nicole. "I get this feeling of deja vu."

"I do as well. I hope this is the last time we have to do anything like this."

He drove the van to Handsworth, and she followed behind in her car. It was still raining. There was no one about when he set fire to the van next to some waste ground. There was a mattress in the back of the van and a duvet, and it spewed out black smoke.

He climbed into her car, and she drove back home. He put in a CD of the Beatles and watched the wipers swish back and forth. He was in pain and would be for days, but it was a small price to pay. He glanced at her. She looked tired. "It's all over."

"Yes. It's such a relief. We can now get on with our lives."

"I put our guns and their guns in the back of the van," he said.

"Did you wipe them? she asked.

"Yes. What's this house like in Dorridge?"

"It's beautiful. It's just like the house I want when I get married."

"When we get married," he said.

She smiled. "When we get married."

She pulled up in her drive. It had stopped raining, and there was a rainbow over her house.

"What a beautiful rainbow," she said. She climbed out of her car and stood looking at the rainbow.

He climbed out of the car and stood by her side. "Do you know what the rainbow means?"

"No. What?"

"It means that it's stopped raining and that the sun's about to come out."

She smiled. "I assume you mean metaphorically, and I pray that you're right."

"I am right," he said. "I know about these things."

They held hands and walked into the house to begin their life together.